'When I was very young,' Ned said, adding with the tact that Ione admired more every moment, 'much younger than you are now, my dad used to sing a song. As I recall, the words of this song went' – and he began to sing in a soft, tuneless voice:

> *'You've got to have money in the bank, Frank.*
> *You've got to have money to start.*
> *When you have money in the bank, Frank,*
> *I'll give you my heart.*

'And that, unfortunately, is how the lady feels.'
'I see,' said Ione . . .

www.kidsatrandomhouse.co.uk

ANNE FINE

On the Summerhouse Steps

CORGI BOOKS

ON THE SUMMERHOUSE STEPS
A CORGI BOOK 0 552 55269 0
978 0 552 55269 1 (from January 2007)

First published in this edition in Great Britain by Corgi Books,
an imprint of Random House Children's Books

This edition copyright © Anne Fine, 2006

Originally published as two separate titles:
THE SUMMER-HOUSE LOON
First published in Great Britain in 1978 by Methuen Children's Books
Copyright © Anne Fine, 1978
THE OTHER DARKER NED
First published in Great Britain in 1979 by Methuen Children's Books
Copyright © Anne Fine, 1979

The right of Anne Fine to be identified as the author of this work
has been asserted in accordance with the Copyright,
Designs and Patents Act 1988.

Papers used by Random House Children's Books are natural, recyclable
products made from wood grown in sustainable forests.
The manufacturing processes conform to the environmental regulations
of the country of origin.

Set in 12/16pt Gioconda by
Falcon Oast Graphic Art Ltd.

Corgi Books are published by Random House Children's Books,
61–63 Uxbridge Road, London W5 5SA,
a division of The Random House Group Ltd,
in Australia by Random House Australia (Pty) Ltd,
20 Alfred Street, Milsons Point, Sydney, NSW 2061, Australia,
in New Zealand by Random House New Zealand Ltd,
18 Poland Road, Glenfield, Auckland 10, New Zealand,
and in South Africa by Random House (Pty) Ltd,
Isle of Houghton, Corner of Boundary and Carse O'Gowrie Roads,
Houghton 2198, South Africa

THE RANDOM HOUSE GROUP Limited Reg. No. 954009
www.kidsatrandomhouse.co.uk

A CIP catalogue record for this book is available from the British Library.

Printed and bound in Great Britain by
Cox & Wyman Ltd, Reading, Berkshire

*For my mother and father
&
Ruth M. Marsden*

Part One

Chapter 1

Ione sat cross-legged on the summerhouse floor, tracing patterns with her fingertips on the cool grey flagstones. She was thinking about resolutions – her summer holiday resolutions, which she was just about to make.

The summerhouse was at the far, tangly end of the garden, way away across the lawn from the house. It was octagonal and tall, like an over-starched tea cosy. Its sides were latticed, made of thin strips of wood nailed across one another diagonally. They were not glassed, so they let in the sun or the wind or the rain.

On this particular evening, though, it was warm, without even a breeze; and the rays of the sinking sun gleamed steadily through the diamond-shaped holes, reflecting them again, but pink this time, on the pitted stone floor. The shapes furthest from Ione, near the sun's side, were squat and close, like honeycomb; but those where she sat, dead in the centre of the summerhouse, under the glassed-over top which supported the rusting weather vane, were long and elegant diamonds, more like arrows pointing both ways.

'Lozenges,' Ione said to herself. 'Like lozenges.'

She found great difficulty in making resolutions of any sort, even though she did it so often. Firstly, she found it hard to keep her mind on the subject; and secondly, she never knew how high a standard to set for herself. After all, she did not wish to be *perfectly* perfect.

She remembered that at the beginning of last term she had resolved three things.

The first had been to do her homework on the night that it was given, neatly and well. This resolution had lasted almost until half term. After that, she had had to renew it about every second Monday morning until the last week of the term, when she hadn't bothered, since nothing mattered except the dancing display and the swimming competition.

The second resolution had divided into two halves: not to tease the biology teacher, who was called Miss Smith; and not to tease her father's guide dog, who was called Mandy.

It was, she soon found, easy enough not to tease Mandy. Ione had only fallen into the habit through boredom in any case; and once the first few days of ignoring Mandy were over, Ione had decided that the old dog was more of a bore herself than the boredom that had led Ione into teasing her in the first place.

It had been a lot harder, at the start, not to tease Miss Smith. But then, during only the second week of term, Miss Smith had squashed Ione flat by suggesting haughtily that perhaps the rest of the class found Ione's persistent comments and feeble jokes as irritating and unamusing as she did herself. Ione could still remember how hot her cheeks felt, and how everyone, even her closest friends, had giggled so meanly. She had been cold and reserved in biology from that moment on; and until the end of the term she never once put up her hand, even when she was sure that she knew the right answer, and no one else did.

So that resolution had, in a sense, been kept *for* her as well as *by* her; but at least it had been kept.

The last resolution had been to read to her

father whenever she knew that he really needed her help.

Ione's father was blind. He was a university professor, who also wrote history books and articles. Mounds of papers came for him in every post, and his study was piled high with thick, heavy files, covered in brown wrapping paper. Most of these he could read for himself, using his fingertips, because they were written in braille, and his fingers ran over the little dots punched in patterns on the paper almost as quickly as Ione herself could read normal black printed alphabet letters with her eyes.

He also had an enormous old brailling machine, two tape recorders and the most amazing talking computer. It could read almost every sort of print fed into its scanner, and spat the words out in a creepy machine-like voice. If Professor Muffet was thinking hard about every sentence he gave it to read, he could make it read slowly. But if he was rushing through, trying to find a particular passage he remembered, he could switch it to talk so fast that Ione could barely make out a word, though the voice only went faster, and never shot up high, like in cartoons, or music played at the wrong speed.

Professor Muffet had a secretary, too: Miss Hope from the agency, who came most days to help so Ione's father could work on his books and articles. Miss Hope was tall and thin, and not very dependable. Her mother was blind, which was why, although Miss Hope was sighted herself, she had once learned braille. Miss Hope was trying to teach Ione braille as well; but with her school-work, Ione didn't seem to have much time, and wasn't getting on too well.

So with all this equipment – although you couldn't really call Miss Hope equipment – Ione's father managed very well. But whenever scruffily written letters from other professors arrived in the early morning post, Professor Muffet would ask Ione over breakfast to take a look to see if there was anything in them at all about Sardinia, or Early Trade Routes, and if there was then he would twist about excitedly on his chair, wafting toast crumbs all over the carpet and Mandy, and say to Ione as casually as he could manage, 'Miss Hope will find time...but if you're not doing anything until the bus comes...perhaps just a paragraph?' Then he would trail off, waiting hope-fully for her to reply.

And mostly she did read at least a couple of

paragraphs out for him before it was time to rush off to catch the bus, although some of the words and the names were impossibly difficult, and what little she understood of the letters seemed awfully boring.

But sometimes she got up from the breakfast table in a hurry, and said she had promised to meet Josephine early at school, or forgotten to feed Mandy or had some homework to finish before she left.

Then he would say cheerfully, 'Oh, well. It can wait. I don't mind. You rush off.'

But she knew that he did mind really, because sometimes Miss Hope was awfully late, and sometimes she even phoned to say she couldn't come at all. So Professor Muffet had to sit all day, wondering what was in the letter that he so much wanted to read.

And so she had made that her third resolution. Had she kept it? She thought she had done much better than before. But she had sometimes told the same old lies to escape. It was only a half-keep really.

So. Three resolutions, and what was the score? One just over half; one almost completely; one better than ever before, but still not good enough to stop her feeling guilty. You could, if you were generous with yourself, call it three passes; but Ione had her doubts.

She ran her finger round and round a pink diamond, still thinking hard. The sun had sunk almost into the hedge now, and though the diamonds were getting longer and longer, their pink was fading fast. But still she sat and thought.

Ione wondered if there was any real *point* in making resolutions. Perhaps she would have behaved in just the same way all last term whether she had made them or not. Perhaps there was no point in going to any trouble making new ones for these summer holidays. She could try drifting through, day by day, and seeing what happened. Perhaps that was what other people did.

Maybe she was the only person in the world who ever made resolutions – except on New Year's Eve, when everybody made them, even her father. It would be nice to know where she stood about this. It would be good if there were some-one she could ask.

Ione did not often wish that she still had a mother. But that summer evening, as the hedge ate up the last splodge of sun, and the last pink diamond on the summerhouse floor shrank neatly into itself and disappeared, she wished for all the world that she still did.

She said, without realizing that she was saying it aloud, 'Maybe I am the only person in the world who wants to be different from what I am.'

Chapter 2

'I doubt that.'

A deep, pleasant voice sounded right behind Ione.

'Indeed, I know for a fact that it's not the case. I, too, think the same quite often.' The voice broke off for a second's thought, and then added, 'Though I don't think it in quite the same way as you do, grammatically.'

Ione had swung round, astonished, when she first heard the strange voice. Now she was staring, wide-eyed, at the interloper as, standing calmly on the summerhouse steps, he stared steadily back at her.

He saw a slim, small girl with shredded-looking hair. She was wearing a shirt which was far too big for her, and a pair of jeans. He couldn't make out the colour of her eyes because of the fringe that fell over them. Her jeans were streaked with slimy-looking grass stains, as though she'd been kneeling on the edge of a damp lawn, weeding flower beds. He had no idea at all how old she was.

She saw, in spite of her fringe, the tallest young man she could have imagined, now leaning comfortably against the rickety wooden doorpost behind her, his grave, long face half in shadow. She thought he must be at least twenty years old. He was thin, and dressed, like her, in blue jeans. His shirt was grubby and a jacket dangled from his fingers behind his back, collecting cobwebs off the doorpost.

He looked as though he had been leaning there, inside the summerhouse, for hours.

'You eavesdropped,' she accused him, hot with embarrassment. 'You were listening to every word I said.'

'True,' he said. 'Though you only said one thing, apart from "lozenges", which didn't really count. I can't *think* what you've been thinking about, all this while.'

He stared around the summerhouse. In one of its eight corners was spread the tattered remains of an ancient web. The spider was long since gone, but the web was enormous. He smiled at it in admiration. Then he turned back to Ione, still smiling. 'You must be a great thinker,' he told her. 'Sitting so still for so long. Anyone else would have gone home for tea *ages* ago.'

'Why haven't you, then?' she countered. 'And what are you doing in our garden?' She finished up fiercely, 'Who *are* you?'

The moment she said it, she realized how much she must have sounded like the snooty Caterpillar who sat on the mushroom in *Alice in Wonderland*, smoking his hookah and asking Alice in such a haughty, off-putting way, 'Who are *you*?'

And, the moment after, she realized that he was thinking exactly the same thing. She saw his face begin to crumple into another smile. Then, to her great relief, before it fully happened, he set his face solemnly again.

And from that moment, because he hadn't teased her when he could have done, and clearly would have liked to, she liked him – hugely and for ever.

'But what are you doing in our summerhouse?' she persisted.

'I am trespassing,' he said simply, and pulled thoughtfully at his ear.

13

Ione didn't know what to say. Neither did he, so they stared at one another a little while longer. Then the interloper began to wriggle untidily into his jacket as though he were about to leave. Ione suddenly knew two things, both at the same time. She knew he was *too* thin, probably from not eating properly and regularly; and she knew he was very unhappy about something.

So she spoke to him again, out of kindness. And at that very moment he spoke to her again, out of curiosity.

'What is your name?' she asked him.

'What *were* you thinking about?' he asked her.

He answered first. His was, after all, much the easier question to answer.

'My name is Ned Hump,' he told her.

She admired the way he said it, so straightforwardly and unapologetically. And his name was almost as bad as hers. Ione was always embarrassed when she had to say her own name to people, especially to strangers. She usually mumbled it out in such a mangled way the first time that she had to go through the agony again.

She decided to be equally forthright with him.

'I was wishing that I had a mother again,' Ione

said. She added defensively, 'I don't wish it very often, but sometimes I do.'

Ned Hump stared at her gravely for a long, long while. Then he said, 'It works both ways, you know. It works exactly the same way backwards, if that makes it any better. People who *do* have mothers sometimes wish they hadn't. They don't wish it often, either; but sometimes they do.'

It did make it better for her. It made it a whole lot better. She felt very grateful to him.

Meanwhile, he had fallen into another of his long, ear-tugging silences. Ione was already beginning to get used to them. So while he gazed moodily over her head, as if she weren't there at all, and out through the summerhouse latticework towards the house beyond, she studied the spangles and circles on his shirt.

There were twice as many pink spangles as there were orange circles, except for round the collar, where the circles seemed to be fraying faster than the spangles. She wondered who on earth had given it to him. It was not the sort of shirt an aunt would buy. She could only suppose he had bought it himself.

She wondered if he trespassed often in her garden, or if this were the first time. Perhaps he was dangerous. He was certainly a little odd. She thought again how he was far too thin.

She wondered if she dare invite him in for tea, since he looked so hungry. Maybe he was one of her father's students, and had a mean landlady who gave him meals that were not nearly nourishing enough for someone of his height. He was so tall, he looked as though he ought to eat a lot.

At long last, he broke his own silence.

'I, too, have my problems,' he told her.

He let his knees buckle beneath him and his body fold down like an old-fashioned clothes horse, until he was sitting on the floor at her side.

'I am in love with Caroline,' he said tragically.

'Caroline?'

'Caroline Hope,' he explained irritably. Then he added, just as irritably, Ione thought, 'I *adore* her.'

'Miss Hope,' said Ione, understanding at last.

'You know her?' he asked. 'Of course you do. You live here. She works here.' Light was dawning visibly on his face. 'You must be Professor Muffet's daughter.' He thought about this. 'If he has one, that is,' he felt obliged to add. 'And that's how you know Miss Hope,' he concluded triumphantly.

'She works for Dad,' Ione explained. 'She's really good at braille. She can even do it while he stands over her and dictates.' She noticed the stranger was once again staring over her head, and out through the summerhouse latticework. She thought perhaps it was because he was not understanding.

'She transcribes,' she said. 'That means she can turn braille into normal writing. Perhaps you didn't know that?'

'I did,' he said, his attention recalled. Then, seeing her face drop because she felt so foolish, he added quickly: 'But purely by chance. I met the word in a book only a few weeks ago.'

Ione smiled at him. He had tact, and tact always made everyone feel better. It suddenly occurred to her that she might make tact her only summer holiday resolution.

And once this decision was made, she felt as though a weight had been lifted from her mind. She felt carefree. She smiled at him again, even more warmly. It was the second thing he had made her feel better about, already.

But he didn't seem to notice her pleasure. His eyes were straying again.

'Miss Hope refuses to marry me.' Ned Hump

continued with his explanation of his problems. 'She refuses frequently and point-blank. I am forever proposing to her. I propose all but daily. And she is forever being nasty to me in return. She's nasty to me whenever she gets the chance – which is at least once a day.'

'Perhaps she gets bored with all your proposals?'

'I don't think so,' said Ned Hump. 'After all, if she were bored, she need only accept my offer once, and the whole repetitive process could come to a timely end. I should never have to ask her again.'

'Unless you divorced,' said Ione.

Ned Hump stared at Ione, trying to digest this. Then he said politely: 'Quite.'

'Perhaps she wants to marry someone else,' suggested Ione, trying to be a little more practical. 'My father, for example. She's always nice enough to him.'

'I don't think so,' said Ned Hump again. 'Much as I respect your father and his work – though, Lord knows, I disagree with every single word he says about the Early Sardinian Trade Routes – I don't think Caroline Hope would wish to marry him. Or, if she did, it would be from sheer contrariness on her part. She is in love with *me*.'

'If she loved you, she'd marry you,' Ione
pointed out, still trying to be practical.

'There are certain aspects of the warped
character of Miss Caroline Hope that have clearly
escaped you up till now,' Ned Hump told Ione.
'For one thing, she has Notions. She has Notions
about Roofs Over Heads, and Good Starts In Life,
and Little Somethings Put Away In Case Of Rainy
Days, and so on and so forth. She's full of Notions.
Chock-a-block full.'

He looked towards Ione for sympathy, but Ione
just looked a little blank. Assuming it was because
she had not fully understood, Ned Hump went
on to explain again, differently and more simply.

'When I was very young,' he said, adding with
the tact that Ione admired more every moment,
'much younger than you are now, my dad used to
sing a song. As I recall, the words of this song went'
– and he began to sing in a soft, tuneless voice:

> '*You've got to have money in the bank,
>   Frank.*
> *You've got to have money to start.*
> *When you have money in the bank, Frank,*
> *I'll give you my heart.*

'And that, unfortunately, is how the lady feels.'

'I see,' said Ione.

And this time she did.

She took a deep breath. 'Would you like to come in for tea?' she invited him.

He, in his turn, took a deep breath. He narrowed his eyes.

'Must I meet *her*?' he asked in a voice brimming with suspicion. 'I don't think I could face it. I've had a basinful of her nastiness already today.'

Ione used tact. It came easily to her, she found. She wondered if it were the same sort of skill as telling lies, which she was also very good at.

'No,' she reassured him. 'You needn't meet her at all. We could have our tea alone in the kitchen. Miss Hope always stays with my dad in the study.'

She saw that he was still hesitating, still unconvinced.

'There's chocolate fudge cake left over from yesterday,' she tempted him. They always had chocolate fudge cake on her last day of term.

He was lost.

Scrambling to his feet, he stretched out a hand to her.

'Come, my lady,' he said.

She took his hand and rose with as much grace as she could muster. She knew that he had badly wanted to say, 'Come, Miss Muffet,' and had controlled himself at the very last moment. She thought that was very kind of him as she suffered from her name a lot.

'My name's Ione,' she told him, as clearly and as unashamedly as he had told her his before.

'I was hoping you'd mention it,' he said. 'It seemed a little late in our flourishing relationship just brutally to ask.'

They crossed the lawn side by side, until they reached the sundial. Here, he stopped to walk round it twice, reading the inscription aloud as he circled it.

'*Seize the present moment,*' he read out, in a sing-song voice. '*The evening hour is nigh.*'

'That's always been another of my problems,' she heard him mutter. Then he strode off again in the direction of the back door.

It suddenly occurred to her that he knew their garden pretty well.

Chapter 3

It wasn't one of Mrs Phipps's days to help in the house, and the kitchen table was still cluttered with lunch things that Ione hadn't yet cleared away.

A few droopy bits of lettuce lay in the salad bowl and lumps of potato were stuck to plates that hadn't yet been put on the draining board, out of the way. There was a shallow pool of fruit juice under the pepper mill, and an aspirin just on the edge, looking a little like a tiny white boat about to be launched on a trip to a monster lighthouse.

The floor, however, looked fairly clean. Mandy had clearly had a quick lick round before she went off to the study for her afternoon sleep.

Ned Hump didn't seem to notice squalor. He just rooted around in the larder until he found the right cake tin. There were several in there, stacked in a tottery pile in one corner; but most were empty. He pulled out the right one, and sat down at the table, out of Ione's way, as he munched his way through the cake he had found. Ione was relieved he did not seem to be the bread-and-butter-first sort. She always cut the loaf crooked, especially if, like today's, it was very fresh.

Ione began to set a tray for her father and Miss Hope. She tried, as she did it, to think of Miss Hope as Caroline; but it wasn't too easy, and she'd never tried it before. She thought that Miss Hope might even decide to change her name to Mrs Hump anyway, and it wasn't worth making the effort of getting used to a change twice.

She filled the teapot and placed beside it a mug, a cup and saucer, milk, sugar and a small plate of coconut biscuits. These were the only treats in the house, now she'd decided to save all the chocolate fudge cake for Ned Hump.

As she picked up the tray, Ned Hump jumped to his feet. He rushed to the door, and swung it open, towering over her as she passed into the hall.

'Forgive me for not carrying it in for you,' he

said, sounding really concerned. 'But I couldn't face the lady at this moment. I have been spurned and insulted enough for one day.'

Ione trailed along the hall, with its faded, fraying carpet and blotchy, damp-stained wallpaper. Since Professor Muffet couldn't see these frays and stains, he did nothing whatever about them, and Ione took them for granted. As long as she could remember, they had always been there.

She reached the far end and pushed the study door open with her shoulder. It was a swing-open door, so that Mandy could get in and out without a great fuss.

When they heard her come in, Miss Hope and Professor Muffet looked up from their work.

'At *last*,' said Professor Muffet. 'We were gasping.'

'How lovely,' said Miss Hope. 'Shall I pour?'

Ione set the tray in front of her, and stepped back to the doorway. She watched as Miss Hope coped, as efficiently as she coped with everything, with the pouring. Miss Hope was a little *too* efficient at times, Ione thought; but for all she tried, standing there in the doorway, she couldn't imagine Miss Hope being nasty to anybody, and especially not to someone as gentle and thoughtful as Ned Hump.

She wondered if perhaps there had been some mistake. Perhaps Miss Hope wasn't Caroline at all, but had a twin sister with that name. Ione tried one more time to think of her as Caroline. It didn't work.

Miss Hope passed Professor Muffet a large, stripy blue mug full of tea. Ione's father always drank out of a mug at home. He hated having to use a cup and saucer. After he'd lifted the cup to sip from it, he always used to forget on which arm of the chair, or on which part of the desk or floor he had left the saucer; and then he had to waste time feeling around for it. Sometimes he gave up and forgot about the saucer entirely and then trod upon it later. So now he always preferred to use a mug.

Professor Muffet was forty-one years old and untidy. He became more and more scruffy-looking as the day went by, not being able to see himself in mirrors as he passed, and straighten himself up a little. He did not have a beard, though it would have been easier – he used an electric razor instead. He usually shaved badly, but more from not trying than from being in-capable. One can, after all, *feel* stubble.

He had been blind since he was six years old.

He could remember all about colours, and what the sea looked like, and so he was easy enough to talk to about that sort of thing. He liked going for long walks, either with Mandy, or with Ione if Mandy was too tired, or with both. And most evenings he played the piano, sometimes late into the night. That was when he most missed his wife, Doris, who used to comment on his wrong notes, and sometimes he even wished he had another wife.

Ione's mother had died when Ione was three years old, so there had always been housekeepers and nannies as long as she could remember. The old ones were always called housekeepers, and known as Mrs Something, and always left because some relation or another had fallen ill, and needed nursing; and the young ones were called nannies, and known by their first names, and always left to get married.

When the last one, a nanny, had left a few months before, Ione had said, '*Must* we have somebody else? Can't we just be us?'

Her father had said, 'She was nice to you, wasn't she? She didn't upset you, I hope.'

'Oh, no,' said Ione. 'It's just that I thought, now I'm so much older, perhaps we could manage, just the two of us.'

Professor Muffet had twiddled his fingers and patted the dog and fingered his tea mug and straightened his files, and wondered if anything anyone *wanted* could possibly be *good* for them, if they were only Ione's age; and at last he had said, 'I'll tell you what. I'll tell you what we'll do. We'll *assume* that we're going to get another nanny. But we'll just not *look* very hard for one. And in the meantime, we'll ask Mrs Phipps to come in from the village more often and do some of the cooking as well as the cleaning. And I'll be even more sensible about getting the food delivered. And in term-time, you must stay at school for lunch. How about that? Will that do?'

'I think that's just right,' Ione had said.

And after that, Ione had even begun to learn to prepare meals, as well as to learn braille. She felt very strongly that she should try and be some help to her father. Sometimes in the past she had been dreadful.

There had been the time, for example, when Ione was five and had first realized that, if she kept dead still and hardly breathed, then Daddy couldn't see or find her, although she could see him. She had often frightened him badly this way when the nanny was on her day off, or in another room.

She still remembered one particular day, one winter's afternoon, when she had pushed over a tea trolley from running too fast.

There had been the most enormous, resounding crash. Splinters of shattered glass and pieces of broken teacups had sprayed far and wide over the carpet. Sugar had dredged the sofa cushions. Tea-leaves had bespattered the curtains. It had all been a dreadful mess, and she knew she was to blame for not looking where she was running.

She had shrunk back into the curtains, held her breath and frozen.

'Ione!' her father had shouted. 'Ione – are you all right?'

But she was terrified because she had broken so many things and spilt so much tea onto everything, and she kept quite, quite still, rigid with fear.

Panicking, her father had dropped onto his knees amid the broken crockery and the damp patches on the carpet. He had felt frantically around on the floor, trying to find her, calling her name all the time. He thought she must have hurt herself badly, and perhaps be lying somewhere out of reach, unconscious.

And she became more and more frightened by his strange behaviour. She was, after all, only five. She had shrunk back further and further into the curtains, as silent as a ghost.

Suddenly, he had seemed to despair of ever finding her.

'Ione,' he had whispered. 'Please, love . . .'

She had let out her breath then, and he had heard and reached out for her. He had pulled her into his arms, and stood up and carried her, trembling all over, to the big red leather chair. And while she had cried and cried, he had stroked her hair and whispered to her that it didn't matter at all, not one bit, until the nanny at last came in from the garden, where she had been rescuing some washing from the rain, and had cleared up the mess in no time at all.

Ione had never been as bad as that again. But even after all these years she had been surprised when her father agreed not to look terribly hard for a new nanny. Ione knew full well that if you didn't look terribly hard, you never found one at all.

Now Miss Hope, teapot in hand and floppy earrings swaying, was smiling in her usual friendly fashion towards Ione, who was still lurking in the doorway.

'Where's your cup?' Miss Hope asked. 'Aren't you joining us today?'

'I don't think so, thank you,' said Ione. 'I think I'd better go and give Mandy some fresh water. I think she's been without for most of the day.'

For all her doubts about the morals of lying, Ione was most accomplished at the art.

By the time she returned to the kitchen, Ned Hump had ploughed his way through all but the last of the fudge cake. This one slice, after some thought and a considerable act of will, he had placed on a nearby plate, and left for his hostess.

He was sitting sunk in gloom, with his head bent, shredding the silver foil in which the cake had been wrapped, and letting the pieces drop to the floor, where they rustled in the draught from the door.

Ione went round the table and stood on the other side, facing him.

'Coffee's easier . . .' she said hopefully. (There was only one teapot.)

'I'd *much* prefer coffee,' he said helpfully, though his voice sounded downcast.

Ione put more water into the kettle, and switched it on again.

'It must be hateful to be in love,' she said, spooning coffee granules into mugs.

'Hateful,' he agreed. 'Especially when one has the misfortune to love an old bat like her.'

Ione stared.

'Do you wish you'd never met her?' she asked, at last.

'No,' he said. 'But that's love for you.'

'She must drive you mad.'

'She does.'

Ione poured boiling water into the mugs. 'She does Dad, too,' she said soothingly.

Ned Hump lifted his head. He did not look soothed. He looked confused and anxious.

'I beg your pardon?' he said.

'She drives my father mad, too,' Ione repeated.

'Ah, yes,' said Ned Hump, and relapsed into being downcast. He buried his nose into his coffee mug, then lifted it out again.

'Why?' he asked.

'Why what?'

'Why does she drive Professor Muffet mad?'

Ione tried to think of her father as Professor Muffet. She found it even more difficult than thinking of Miss Hope as Caroline. She wondered *why* she always thought of Miss Hope as Miss Hope. Miss Hope couldn't, after all, be older than Ned Hump, and she could think of Ned Hump as Ned with no trouble at all. She tried, just as an experiment, to think of Ned as Mr Hump, and lost herself in a tangle of assorted thoughts.

Patiently, Ned Hump asked his question all over again. '*Why* does Caroline drive your father mad?'

Ione considered.

'He says she's not dependable,' she said.

'He's dead right, she's not.'

'Dad says she's always ringing him up at the last minute, saying she can't come at all; or, if she can, it won't be for hours and hours.'

'He gets that too, does he?' asked Ned, with interest. He seemed to be cheering visibly. 'Why does he put up with it?' He sighed. 'It's not as if he were in love with her too.'

Ione considered. He *might* be. After all, Miss Hope was awfully pretty, though her father only had *her* word for that. And she had a lovely low, chokey voice. But then, her father was far too old for Miss Hope. She decided that the obvious answer must be the right one, after all.

'He *has* to,' she said. 'She's the only person the agency could find when Miss Nettleton left who could transcribe from braille *and* come and live near here so she could come and do it every day.' She drank some of her coffee. 'And Dad says she's very good indeed at the job, and doesn't shuffle all his papers up, out of spite, like the last one did. But she's only good when she's here. And she's so often *not* here. And so Dad gets into rages – goes quite mad, like when he gets letters telling him to hurry up and do things – and he says terrible things about Miss Hope. And then sometimes, when he's really in a rage, he starts on about that loon of a sardine of hers.'

'That *what*?'

Ned Hump was totally baffled.

'That loon of a sardine who lures her away from her work.' Ione reached over the table and cut herself a bit off the last slice of cake.

Ned Hump ran a long finger round and round the rim of his coffee mug, clockwise, dissolving the sugar that had stuck to its edge. He was still baffled.

'I knew she kept a cat,' he said. 'I didn't know she kept a sardine. Especially not an ailing one that she has to stay home and nurse. Indeed I didn't think that *anybody* kept sardines – except in tins, of course, for unexpected guests.'

He began to run a different finger round the rim of his mug, in the other direction. 'You would think,' he said thoughtfully, 'that she would find herself hard pressed to keep her cat from eating the sardine. I imagine cats are partial to sardines.'

He stopped rubbing his mug altogether, and looked up. 'But Caroline Hope was always resourceful,' he concluded. 'If anybody in the world could keep a cat and a sardine in the same flat without a catfight, it would be her.'

He sank his chin into his hands.

'Blast her to bits,' he added, as an afterthought.

Ione had finished chewing her mouthful of cake now and could speak again.

'She doesn't keep sardines at all,' she said. 'Nobody does. They're always dead to begin with.'

'They're not *born* in tins, you know,' said Ned Hump.

'You know what I mean,' said Ione.

Ned Hump lowered his head, as a kind of apology.

Ione went on with her explanation.

'That loon of a sardine is just Dad's nickname for one of his students at the university,' she said.

'He says Miss Hope is always letting him down so that she can rush off, at no notice at all, to parties and films and things with this student. It's the *student* he calls that loon of a sardine.'

Ione was deep into her cake again, so she neither saw the stormclouds of comprehension gathering on Ned Hump's brow, nor noticed the sudden glitter in his eyes. She sailed on, after swallowing, into a deeper and deeper lack of tact.

'Dad calls this student a loon of a sardine because he has' – she took a breath and tried to remember the exact phrase her father always used – 'because he has the most extraordinarily loony views Dad can imagine *anyone* holding on the Early Sardinian Trade Routes. Dad says he sometimes even fears for this student's sanity.'

Ione lifted the last of her cake, and that was when she saw his face. That was when, at long last, the exact phrase rang the exact bell. Early Sardinian Trade Routes. It was the same phrase that Ned Hump had used. It was exactly what he said he disagreed with her father about, when they met in the summerhouse.

Ione's hand froze. Her face went scarlet.

She sat there, unable to move, appalled by her slowness and her lack of tact.

'You . . .' she faltered, at last. '*You're* the *loon*?'

She could hardly believe it. But of course it all fitted in.

Ned Hump rose to his feet.

First she thought he was going to stalk out in a huff, but he just stuck out his hand.

'Meet,' he said, formally. 'Meet your first walking, talking sardine.' He shook her hand. '*Loon* of a sardine, that is,' he corrected himself.

Then he bowed like something out of a tin and she nearly fell off her chair, laughing as loudly as he was.

Chapter 4

They were laughing so merrily that neither of them heard the door's faint click, and the quiet swoosh of draught as it swung open.

Neither of them noticed Professor Muffet standing framed in the doorway, the plate of coconut biscuits in his hand.

Their bout of laughter did, however, finally die away. And it was only then that Professor Muffet spoke.

'Do I hear *two* laughs?' he enquired of the air around him. 'Do I hear, merged companionably, the laughter of my daughter and the laughter of Ned Hump?'

'Oh, Lord,' said Ned Hump. All of a sudden, he looked as though he hadn't laughed in weeks.

'What are you about, young man?' Professor Muffet went on. 'Settled in my kitchen, carousing with my daughter, the evening before your exam?'

'Oh, Lord,' said Ned Hump again. He was totally taken aback. He couldn't think how Professor Muffet had known it was him, solely from hearing his laugh. He was not aware of how skilled Professor Muffet had become at guessing whose voice he was hearing, even in unexpected places and even from a shout or a laugh. Ned might have expected to have his voice recognized in the university, asking a question after a lecture, or offering to take Mandy out for a quick run. But to have his laugh pinned down in a kitchen where he had never been before, and where he had no business to be, put him out rather.

So Ned stared fixedly at the last of the cake, and wondered what he could say. Finally, he said, 'We met in the summerhouse. And now I'm eating your chocolate cake. Your daughter is very kindly feeding me up. Before the ordeal.'

He turned to Ione and added politely, in explanation, 'By the ordeal, I mean my exam. It's tomorrow, at half past three. I don't have to *write* anything – that part was all over last month. But I have to sit in front of a tableful of historians, including your father, and answer their questions on what I did write, last month, without appearing to them to be an idiot. And on this exam tomorrow my whole future depends. Only afterwards will I know if I have a good enough exam result to get a good enough job to get Roofs Over Heads and Good Starts In Life and Little Somethings To Put Away In Case Of Rainy Days, and therefore the hand in marriage of Caroline Hope.'

He listed off Miss Hope's Notions in exactly the same order as he had done before in the summerhouse. Ione thought he must think and worry about them a lot to have them off so pat. She gazed at him, her eyes brimming with pity behind her fringe.

But Professor Muffet leaned against the draining board trying hard not to let his amusement show. The plate of coconut biscuits in his hand slipped into a rather dangerous angle.

Ned Hump looked at the last of the cake even more moodily than before. Clearly, listing the Notions had depressed him. Then, without thinking, for what was left was by rights Ione's, he reached out his hand and took it from the plate. He made deliberate, rounded fingerprints on the chocolate coating, and then inspected them.

'Of course,' he went on bitterly, 'the likelihood

of my doing well tomorrow is not great. I'm told I hold views on the Early Sardinian Trade Routes that shouldn't be held by a sane man; that are unacceptable even to the sparsely informed; that befit only a crank.' He added for the benefit of Ione in case she hadn't understood a word: 'In short, your father already thinks I am an idiot.'

'I'm sure he doesn't,' said Ione with prompt tact.

'I *do*,' said Professor Muffet. 'I am convinced of it.'

Professor Muffet was usually polite, but he had been arguing with Ned Hump about the Early Sardinian Trade Routes for a whole term now, and it was getting to be a very sore point with him. In his agitation, he let the plate in his hand slide even further at an angle, and the coconut biscuits fell off it, one by one.

He didn't notice that the plate had suddenly become a little lighter. His eyes glittered. He was getting on his hobby-horse.

'Hump here holds that Gesualdo of Punta Lamormara who, I would remind you, Ione, would only have been *seven years old* at the time in question—'

Ione looked blankly at her father.

'*Only* if you take Punkle's calculation of the year of Gesualdo's birth to be the correct one,' put in Ned Hump.

'Which you don't?'

'Which I don't.'

'Then you're an idiot,' said Ione's father triumphantly, as though his point had been proved beyond all doubt. 'You're totally insane. And what are you doing in my kitchen, you madman?'

But Ned Hump didn't reply to this taunt. He had suddenly dived headlong under the table and was cowering behind Ione's knees, clutching at her jeans, trying desperately to hide every last lanky bit of himself as Miss Caroline Hope appeared in the doorway.

She'd come to see what was happening, and why the professor had been away so long just looking for chocolate fudge cake.

As she came in, she took the empty plate from his hand and put it safely on the draining board, out of the way.

'Did you eat *all* of them?' she asked him, with interest. 'Every last one? I thought you didn't care for them, either. I thought that was why you came back here. To see if there was cake.'

She turned to Ione. 'Isn't there any left over from yesterday?' She caught sight of the last of the crumbs on the plate on the table.

'Goodness, you glutton,' said Miss Hope to Ione. 'You've pigged it all. And there was masses.'

A choking noise sounded underneath the table. Ione coughed to try and disguise it, but Miss Hope was not an idiot.

She bent down low and peered under the table.

'Why, Ned,' she said, sweet as sugared poison. 'How kind of you to crawl in.'

'Oh, Lord.' Ned Hump's voice wafted up from somewhere beneath Ione. Then he despaired and clambered out.

'Oh, Lord.' Professor Muffet's voice wafted over from where, weak from laughing, he was clutching the draining board for support. And *he* was only *imagining* the scene.

Blotches of chocolate had worked their way all over Ned Hump's unusual shirt, making the pattern even more bizarre.

Miss Hope glared venomously at Ned Hump. 'What are you doing in this house, you meddlesome, nosy moron?' she demanded.

Ione stared, astonished, at Miss Hope. She was quite a different person. All vague thoughts of possible twin sisters vanished from Ione's brain. This was the Miss Hope she knew, and yet this was nastiness indeed – sheer, neat nastiness.

Ione saw for the first time what Ned meant when he said to her that he had had a basinful of the lady already that day.

Ione turned her eyes curiously onto Ned. He was looking defeated and gormless, pulling threads from the frayed ends of his shirt cuffs, and then wrapping them tightly round his finger-tips. From time to time, his large, spaniel's eyes looked up and shone mournfully at his beloved.

Ione acted. She remembered that, come what may, Ned loved Caroline. So she acted.

'Mandy chased him in here,' she said decisively. 'She must have got out of the garden. And he was just walking down the road, and Mandy went mad, he says, quite berserk, and chased him in through the gate and over the lawn. He was scared she might bite him so he banged on the kitchen door, and I let him in, and we barricaded the door against Mandy, but threw her some chocolate cake to calm her down.'

She stopped. She saw the blatant disbelief in Miss Hope's ice-hard eyes. Ione finished up, a little lamely, 'We think that it was because Ned had been near a terrier – perhaps near Mrs Phipps's terrier further up the hill, and somehow got the smell of terrier onto his jeans. Mandy *hates* terriers.'

Ione's voice died away again. It never did to add too much icing to a lie.

But she needn't have bothered herself in the first place. Miss Hope had clearly not believed a single word of the tale.

'That dog,' said Miss Hope icily, 'is so fat that she could no more chase Ned Hump than fly.'

Ione was momentarily defeated. But since Ned still appeared to be incapable of defending himself, she set off on another rescue tactic. This time, she tried distraction.

'Mandy *is* fat,' she admitted, gabbling cheerfully, as though she thought that by the sheer speed of her voice alone she could carry all their minds far from the issue under discussion. 'Dad tried to put her on a diet once, just before you came, Miss Hope. He only let her eat one meal a day, and no scraps. So we had to keep the kitchen floor well swept all the time. It was such a bother, Mrs Phipps swore that she'd leave. But Mandy didn't get any thinner. She just got fearfully hungry and bad-tempered, and refused to lead Dad all the way to the bus stop.'

She turned to her father for support; but he could give her none. He was almost doubled up with laughter. So Ione carried on alone.

'*Yes*, you do. You remember. She began stopping halfway up Hanger's Hill and you couldn't budge her, not one inch, because she was such a tub; and the bus driver only stopped because he *knew* you, and then after a week or so, the driver said you'd *have* to get Mandy off the diet, or whatever it was that was making her act so oddly, because the company had told him that he mustn't stop the bus for you on that hill any more, because it was a bend and *far* too dangerous, and the lives of the other passengers were at risk. So *you* said that since there were only two other regular passengers on that bus any how, and one of those was only . . .'

Ned Hump had laid a hand gently on Ione's shoulder.

'It's no use,' he told her. 'I've tried it often enough myself. It doesn't work. Nothing does. Nothing works with her when she's in a mood.'

Miss Hope's eyes flashed green fire.

'Ooooh!' she choked. 'You tiny-minded, pea-brained *pin-head*! You think you're so *noble*, don't you? That's what gets me. And yet you won't do *one tiny thing* for me. You say you love me, and yet you won't do *one tiny thing.*'

'One tiny thing?' Ned shouted back. 'One tiny thing!' His voice reached a shriek. '"*My whole fortune's fee*", more like.' He paused to let his voice come down an octave, then swung round to face his tutor.

Professor Muffet heard him move, and tried to put his face straight.

Livid with outrage, Ned told Professor Muffet, 'She wants me to *perjure* myself, to *appease*, to *conform*. She wants me, tomorrow, to *sell my soul.* She wants me to tell giant great lies about what I believe and don't believe, about the Early Sardinian Trade Routes, just so, *if* we ever do get married – and I'm fast going *off* the idea – then I'll have a good degree, so I'll get a good job like hers so we'll be able to buy a better house and fill it with fridges and all that other rubbish.'

Caroline shrieked at him then, outraged in her turn.

'It isn't fridges,' she cried, almost in tears of fury. 'I never even *mentioned* a fridge. It's your stupid *babies* I'm worried about, Ned Hump. I've told you before, and I'll tell you again and again and again, I am *not* having your babies and living under a *hedge*.'

There fell, between the two of them, the silence of exhaustion. And not for the first time either.

Professor Muffet pulled himself together and stepped into the large, social hole that had been dug in his kitchen.

'Ione,' he said, 'can you remember what I did with the whisky bottle?'

'Yes, I can,' said Ione. 'You hid it from Aunt Alice. You hid it in one of your Wellington boots.'

He asked her where they were, but she didn't answer. She was miles away, thinking. She was thinking that Miss Hope had quite a point, when you thought about it. Ione wouldn't care to bring up a family of babies under a hedge, either. They would be almost *bound* to catch pneumonia and die.

'So,' said Ione's father, with a large and obvious sigh, 'Hump and I will go to my study. Kindly keep us undisturbed until we emerge. If we do nothing else before night falls, we shall settle this question of the Early Sardinian Trade Routes for once and for all. Follow me, Hump.'

Ned followed him, though reluctantly. They had been arguing about the Early Sardinian Trade

Routes all term, and he was fed up with it all too.

But as he passed Ione, he brightened up enough to blow her a kiss. And as he passed Miss Hope, he said out of the corner of his mouth, 'Marry me, you stubborn old bat, and be my only sweet love foreverandevermore.'

'Push off, Ned,' said Miss Hope.

Ned stuck out his large tongue at her, and shambled off after Professor Muffet.

Ione watched him go. She wondered if even she might, just now and then, find him a little bit trying.

Chapter 5

Left alone together, Ione and Miss Hope surveyed the wreckage on the kitchen table and on the floor. Then they sat down.

'I think,' said Ione, surprising herself with her frankness, 'I think that *I* would marry him even if I did have to live under a hedge. He's more lovely than not.'

Miss Hope yawned. Her temper had quite passed over, leaving her as sunny as usual.

'Do you have any other drink in the house?' she asked. 'Anything that isn't closeted in with those two, I mean. Cooking sherry, or something? I really don't see why they should be the only ones to have a drink, I really don't.'

'I know we have cooking sherry,' said Ione, 'because we use it for trifles when Aunt Alice comes. Aunt Alice loves trifles, and Mrs Phipps always puts loads of sherry in them so that Aunt Alice will go off to sleep after lunch and leave her in peace.' She went into the larder and began looking for it. 'But it's probably ancient by now,' she added. 'Aunt Alice hasn't been for ages.'

'It keeps,' said Caroline. 'Sometimes it even improves.'

'I've never drunk before,' said Ione. 'Except at Christmas and New Year, and things like that.'

'Oh, well,' said Miss Hope philosophically, 'better to start off on a life of vice with me than with' – she paused, and then finished – 'than with anyone less dependable.'

'Dad doesn't think you're at all dependable,' said Ione, tact slipping. 'And neither does Ned.'

She searched around the pantry shelves and felt behind the breakfast cereals, until she found, behind the gravy-browning bottle and the soy sauce, the cooking-sherry bottle. It was covered with dust, and quite full, though the label was peeling on one side.

They drank the sherry from mugs. It seemed simpler, if not as elegant, as drinking out of glasses. Besides, the sherry glasses were in the study, from which loud, aggressive noises had begun to issue. It sounded as though the question of the Early Sardinian Trade Routes was being very thoroughly thrashed out.

Ione looked at her watch. It was a quarter past eight.

Ione looked at her watch. It was whizzing round and round and round. The face was spinning in one direction, and the numbers were spinning in the other. They were not spinning fast, but fast enough not to be able to pin down long enough to read. And the big and little hands seemed temporarily to have disappeared.

'What time is it?' she asked.

Miss Hope, who had, during Ione's mugful of sherry, inexplicably and without any warning at all turned into being Caroline, narrowed her dark green eyes. Being more practised in drinking than Ione, she did not even attempt to tell the time from her tiny gold wristwatch, but peered through drooping eyelids at the large wall clock.

'It is a quarter past midnight,' she said.

'Never!' Ione said. She was astonished.

They had been playing poker, which Caroline had just taught her, for four whole hours, using a pack of cards Caroline found at the back of the spoon drawer. Since there were no matches to be found, they were playing with spoons; and the table was now covered with spoons – apostle spoons, teaspoons, serving spoons, wooden spoons, two ladles, and even an ice-cream dispenser that Ione had found on the larder floor. Caroline was winning. She had won every game so far.

Caroline now said, 'Are they still at it?'

They sat without moving, so that the table stopped rocking and the spoons stopped jangling. From the study still came the sounds that Professor Muffet and Ned Hump had been making all evening, and as they had drunk further and further down the whisky bottle, those sounds had become louder and louder.

As Caroline and Ione had drunk their way further and further down the cooking sherry, they had noticed the noise less and less.

'*Why* won't you marry him?' Ione asked Caroline for at least the tenth time. She found it difficult, with her head as fuzzy as it felt, to remember exactly which questions she *had* asked Caroline, and which she had only *thought* of asking her.

Strangely, she did not seem to remember Caroline's answers at all.

'Why don't I marry him?' Caroline's voice was slurry-furry on top of its usual chokiness. 'I've *told* you. I've told you *over* and *over*. I *will* marry him. Put that ladle back at *once*. It's from *my* pile. I'll marry him *when* he has a job.'

Caroline reached down and picked up a piece of coconut biscuit from where it was wedged, in the handle of the cupboard under the draining board.

'Blast him to bits,' she added, in just the same tone of voice that *he* had used when he wished the same on her.

Ione smiled to herself. She thought that Caroline and Ned would go wonderfully together, married.

Caroline licked the biscuit experimentally. 'Tastes so arid, coconut does,' she said. 'Like the Sahara desert.' She licked it again. 'If you don't like deserts, that is,' she said. 'I mean, if you don't like coconut.'

Suddenly she froze dramatically, one finger raised.

'Sshhh,' she said. 'Listen.'

Ione listened. She felt she could hear her head going round, but that was inside her. Outside her, there was nothing to be heard. Not one sound. Even the spoons had shut up for the moment.

'Jeepers,' muttered Ione. 'Have they killed one another? Are they dead?'

'Dead drunk, more like,' said the more experienced Caroline, and she giggled.

She placed the licked piece of biscuit carefully back on the cupboard handle where she had found it and rose, a little unsteadily, to her feet. With biscuity fingers, she pushed the hair from her eyes, tangling coconut crumbs in her curls.

'We should go and investigate,' she told Ione. 'We should go and see exactly what has happened.'

Caroline led the way down the hall, and Ione stumbled behind her. It was, Ione found, slightly more difficult to walk than to sit at a kitchen table. The walls seemed to surge in, then rush away again. Her feet seemed to want to take off to one side, on their own.

Ione was concentrating so hard on her own somewhat crab-like progress that she didn't notice when Caroline came to a halt, and so she fell heavily against her.

Caroline, being more experienced, held firm.

'The keyhole,' suggested Ione, in a conspiratorial whisper.

'There is none,' Caroline pointed out. 'It is a swing door.'

She spoke slowly and clearly, as though she had to work hard to choose the right words, then say them in exactly the right order and at an equal level of loudness.

Caroline pushed the swing door open a fraction and peered through the crack she had made. She could only see one corner of the room, and neither Ned nor Professor Muffet was, at that moment, in that corner.

Caroline gave a large, dramatic sigh.

She tried to push the door open a fraction more. It wouldn't give. She pushed harder. It remained firm.

On the other side of the door, Mandy was awakening from a deep sleep because of a strange and forceful pressure of cold door on her rump. She tried to ignore it and carry on with her dream, but the pressure increased, colder and more forceful. Mandy came to her senses enough to rise, shake herself and pad off to her other favourite late-night sleeping patch, under the professor's desk.

At that very moment Caroline pushed one last time, even harder.

Since the obstruction had taken itself off, the door swung wide open fast, and Caroline careered into the room, closely followed by Ione, who had been leaning upon her for support.

The two surveyed the room. It seemed to be swaying slightly, but it was definitely empty. The French windows, however, were ajar and the curtains were billowing in the night breeze.

'They must have stepped out for a walk,' said the more experienced Caroline. She picked up the whisky bottle from where it stood on a pile of papers. It left a faint golden ring.

'Empty,' she said. 'And so the walk may well prove all but fatal. Fresh air can be the worst thing after a lot of hard drink.'

'Doesn't it clear your head?' said Ione, who rather wanted to go out to find them. 'I thought that it did.'

'In the end it does,' Caroline admitted. 'But often only after it has made you feel a lot worse first.'

The last two words – the sound of them – seemed to appeal to her greatly. 'Worse forse, worse forse, worse forse,' she sang gently to herself, swaying round in tight little circles, cradling the empty bottle. Her drunkenness from one large mugful of sherry seemed to come over her in waves, unlike Ione's from her small one, which stayed at a steady level of not quite being in control, and feeling things deeply.

'But it's so *nice* out,' said Ione, feeling this deeply. 'There's moonshine and stars all over.' She peered wistfully out of the gap in the French windows.

Caroline giggled again. 'Very well,' she said. 'Very well. *We* shall go out, too. But I warn you it may be dangerous. Just try not to take any breaths.'

They stepped down the few veranda steps onto the lawn. Caroline was still clutching the whisky bottle. Ione was beginning to wonder if Caroline was more experienced, after all, or whether she had just poured into her mug more of the cooking sherry than she had let on.

'Where shall we go?' demanded Caroline. '*You* should know. It's your garden.'

Ione considered.

'We *could* go to the summerhouse,' she suggested. She wanted to find her father and Ned Hump, and thought they might be there. They didn't appear to be anywhere in the shrubbery, from the lack of rustling; and they were nowhere in the open. That only left the summerhouse. 'But,' Ione added dubiously, 'it might be a little scary there at this time of night.' Her mind somersaulted back to earlier that day. 'There might be a stranger lurking there,' she said. 'Like Ned did.'

Caroline giggled. 'A loon,' she said. 'Another loon, under the moon, whom we may meet soon, though it's well past June.'

She seemed to be in a very rhymy mood, Ione thought.

'*I* shall protect you,' said Caroline.

So they plodded carefully over the dew-sodden grass towards the tangly end of the garden. Ione's head was swirling. She felt just a little sick.

But just as they were only a few steps away from the summerhouse, the moon shot out from behind a cloud and lit the whole scene in a glimmering, pale-silver way, and her sickness was forgotten.

Both of them gazed in admiration and wonder. Caroline had never seen the summerhouse before, and Ione had never seen it looking at all like this.

It shimmered. It gleamed. It looked a thousand years old.

'My!' breathed Caroline. 'It has hundreds and hundreds of sides.'

Ione's head was settling now. Caroline had been right, as usual. After you felt worse, you felt better.

'Not hundreds of sides,' she said. 'Don't be silly. It *couldn't* have that many. It has eight. There look more in this weird light, but in fact there are only eight.'

Caroline said, 'There must be at least a dozen.'

Ione said, 'There are exactly eight.'

Caroline insisted, 'There are a dozen.'

Ione said loftily. 'It is octagonal. So there are eight. You can walk round and count if you don't believe me.'

Suddenly, it was very important to Ione that Caroline *should* believe her. This was partly because her mind was placing an exaggerated importance on trivial things because of the sherry, and partly because she was more than a little fed up with being the youngest person in the house and knowing the least. And this she *did* know. The summerhouse had eight sides. It was *her* place. She spent *hours* there. She should know.

'Very well,' said Caroline. 'I shall walk round and count.'

This was easier said than done, since this was the tangly end; but Caroline forced her way bravely through the thorny brambles and the prickly briars, and the stumpy little two-year-old chestnut trees that the man who sometimes came to help with the garden hadn't yet noticed and uprooted.

And on each side of the summerhouse, as she passed by, Caroline delivered a loud thump, counting aloud.

At last, after what seemed to Ione to be a noisy age, she appeared again round to the right, and leaned against the side that Ione was marking by leaning against herself.

Caroline was completely dishevelled. 'You're right,' she panted. 'It has exactly eight sides, and my tights are in shreds.'

Ione giggled, and the moon swam out again even shinier than before, and lit everything around them, almost to brightness.

Ione gasped.

There on the summerhouse door, scored heavily into the paint-flaked wood, was lettering she had never seen before.

'Look,' she whispered, and pointed.

Caroline looked first at Ione's finger, and then

she pulled herself together and looked where Ione was pointing. Then she gasped, too.

'Look what he's *done*,' she whispered back, horrified. 'It'll be there for *ever*.'

He had hacked, in huge, uneven letters, deep into the door's panels, his drunken, heartfelt message:

NED HUMP LOVES CAROLINE. THIS IS MORE THAN TRUE. XXXXX

Caroline stood dead still. Her cheeks went pink. She stretched out her fingers and ran them gently over each letter in turn, whispering the message to herself as she did so. '*Ned Hump loves Caroline. This is more than true. Kiss, kiss, kiss, kiss, kiss.*'

Then she sat down on the step and burst into noisy, sentimental tears.

Ione sat beside her. She wasn't sure why Caroline was crying, so because it was the only thing she could think of to say, and she really meant it, she said, 'How lovely for you.'

Caroline's sobs subsided. Ione had said just the right thing. While Caroline calmed down, Ione gazed round the moonlit tangles. *She* wouldn't

have cried, she thought, if it had been written for
her. Well, maybe she would . . .

Caroline said, 'How lovely for me.' She sat and
giggled.

Once again, the thought crossed Ione's mind
that Caroline might not, perhaps, be nearly as
experienced as she claimed.

They might, Ione thought, have sat there all night,
had not a strange noise suddenly floated across
the lawn towards them.

Ione shook Caroline into quiet.

'Listen,' she said.

Out of the shadowy night came the sound of
singing – tuneless, happy, mindless singing:

> *'Here we go round the sundial bush,*
> *The sundial bush, the sundial bush;*
> *Here we go round the sundial bush,*
> *On a warm and moony evening.'*

Ione dragged Caroline to her feet and along
the path between the brambles to the edge of the
lawn. The moon was still out, and in the eerie
half-light it cast, they saw a strange sight.

Ione's father and Ned Hump had come from

nowhere out into the middle of the lawn. Like two untidy scarecrows suddenly brought to life, they were careering round and round the sundial, holding hands across it to keep one another upright and revolving. And as they wheeled and spun, they howled their warped nursery rhyme out to the moon, over and over again.

Caroline pulled herself together.

'Couple of loons,' she said acidly.

She appeared to be quite put out. Perhaps, Ione thought, after the loving message they had just found, she had imagined Ned to be alone and palely loitering, like the knight-at-arms in the poem.

Caroline turned and took Ione's hand.

'You and I will return to the house,' she said in a distinctly school-mistressy tone of voice that Ione strongly resented. 'We shall find beds and go to sleep.'

She led the way indoors, stepping silently round the edge of the lawn, shrouded by the lilacs, so they wouldn't be noticed, though she took the trouble to walk with her nose in the air, in case they were.

Ione went with her most unwillingly, dragging her feet. She could hardly take her eyes off her father and Ned Hump, dancing their crazy dance. She rustled against all the bushes she could in the hope they would hear and call them over. But both Ned and her father were making so much noise that they could hardly hear each other, let alone anyone else.

Ione stumbled on the steps into the house, from looking backwards over her shoulder, whilst being firmly pulled by Caroline.

Safe in the study, Caroline took her nose out of the air for a second.

'One blind, and one blind drunk,' she said coldly. Then she softened a little. 'Is there any chance your father will hurt himself, Ione?'

Ione tried to think. She found it difficult, with Caroline in all these moods one after another, and standing so close. Ione found Caroline's changes of mood exhausting. No wonder, she thought to herself, no *wonder* Ned Hump is so *thin*.

Finally she suggested, 'We could send Mandy out. Mandy'll keep an eye on him.'

Caroline dug a reluctant Mandy out from under the desk with her foot. 'Wake up, dog,' she said. 'Get out there. Earn your keep.'

Though tipped out onto the carpet like a large grey beachball, Mandy ignored Caroline in the most dignified way she could think of: she pretended that she was still fast asleep.

So Ione tried. She bent down and tickled Mandy's ears. 'Go find Daddy,' she whispered. 'Go to Daddy. Fetch Daddy.'

With a yawn, Mandy pulled herself upright. She licked Ione's nose wetly, mostly in order to snub Caroline, and plodded obediently out of the French windows and over the lawn. She sat down again, still yawning, a little way from the sundial, just out of danger from any passing, flailing limbs, and waited patiently for the lunatic dance to finish.

'What a clever dog she is,' said Ione proudly, watching from the window. The lick had surprised and delighted her.

'Ought to be,' said Caroline. 'Guide dogs cost enough. And they take *ages* to train.' She pushed open the door to the hall. 'Where shall *I* sleep?' she asked. 'I can't possibly drive home.'

Caroline was right. She couldn't possibly drive home. So Ione said, 'There's a spare bed that usually has sheets on, in the attic. It's in the room with a green door, and a very long scratch down the paint. It's a very narrow bed, though.'

'That's quite all right,' said Caroline, nose in

the air again. 'I am quite narrow, too, width-wise.'

They said goodnight on the landing. Ione stumbled into her own bedroom, and Caroline pulled herself, with the help of the banisters, up the attic stairs in search of a green door with a long scratch down the paintwork.

Both of them were tired to death.

Chapter 6

The moon-dance around the sundial came to an abrupt halt. Ned had tripped over one of his feet and fallen over backwards. He lay on the lawn, winded, and stared up at the sky.

'Just look at those *stars*,' he said, in an ecstasy of appreciation. 'Just look at that *moon*.'

Professor Muffet sat down heavily on the other side and lay back on the grass too. He lay face-up, panting. His eyes, like Ned's, were wide open.

'Beautiful,' he agreed. 'Superb.'

He really could see stars, even if he couldn't see the moon. And he could see more stars than Ned, but of a different kind.

'Ned,' said Professor Muffet, when he at last had his breathing under control again, and his mind ground into action. 'Ned, why won't that girl marry you? You're a good lad.'

Deciding it was probably now safe to approach, Mandy crept up on him, sneaking on her belly across the grass, and he made room under his armpit for her damp nose. Mandy curled up tight and close, to try to get warm again, and went back to sleep.

'No job; no money.' Ned's sad reply floated through the half-light. The moon had vanished again, and shadow had taken over from the gleam.

Professor Muffet nodded sagely and brushed a wet blade of grass off his ear. 'But you'll have one and some, one day,' he said.

Ned took time to sort this out. One which? Some what? Ah, yes. One job. Some money. One day. He had a sudden vision of a wallet full of ten-pound notes in his jacket, and lay there intrigued beyond measure.

Meanwhile, Professor Muffet asked, 'What would you like to do most, after you leave next week?'

'Have a baby,' said Ned.

'I beg your pardon?'

'Have Caroline have a baby,' Ned corrected himself hastily.

'Why?'

'I *like* babies,' said Ned. He thought it was a

silly question and was rather surprised at the professor. 'I *want* babies. Lots of them. Cotfuls.'

Professor Muffet thought about all the babies he and Doris used to dream of having. They had hoped for a son, to be called Edward, next.

'What will you call them all?' he asked.

'Caroline,' said Ned.

'Every last one?'

'Every last one.'

'Boys and all?'

'Boys and all.'

'Gracious!'

Mandy woke then, because the damp of the dew was seeping through her fur and into her skin. She tried to wriggle her large rump inside Professor Muffet's jacket. He tried, ineffectually, to fight her off. When the battle had at last been resolved in Mandy's favour, Professor Muffet said, 'Ned, I've thought of a solution to your problem.'

Ned jerked himself upright. But his head gave a sickening reel, so he lay down again, gently, to quieten it.

'What?' he asked weakly.

'Get a job. Earn some money.'

Ned thought about this. It seemed watertight. The vision of the full wallet came over him again.

Then he saw the flaw. He said, 'But I'm only interested in doing history.'

'Become an historian, then. Like I am.'

Ned thought about this, too. Then he said, 'I should need to get a very good exam result though, shouldn't I? And I won't. Because to-morrow afternoon, you and the rest of the examiners are going to ask me why I wrote what I did in that essay about the Early Sardinian Trade Routes. And so the fact that I still hold these disreputable views will come to light and I shan't get a very good result. And so all will be lost. Nobody on this earth will consider giving me a job as a historian. And so Caroline Hope will reject me for the hundred and oneth and last time, and we shall never have any baby Carolines in cots.'

His voice trailed away sadly. To cheer himself, he became fascinated in the stars overhead, which seemed to be performing, just for him, a speedy and complicated square-dance.

There was a very long silence. For a while, not even Professor Muffet could think of a way out of this one.

Then, at last, he did.

'Ned,' he said, 'I've thought of a solution to this problem, too.'

'What?' said Ned.

'You could dissemble.'

'What?'

'Dissemble. Not to mince words, tell a few whoppers. Hide your disreputable views on the Early Sardinian Trade Routes. Pretend that extraordinary essay you wrote was all a mistake, a brainstorm brought on by the strain of exams. Pretend you're a sane man again.'

The more Professor Muffet thought about it, the simpler it seemed. He carried on, saying a little more than he should have in his determination to persuade Ned.

'You will pass with Honours, and may even be offered a job at this very university because Higgins is having to leave to have a long rest. His doctor has ordered it. So we need someone next term to help with all the teaching, and if you were to get this job, you'd be accepted by Miss Hope. And you and she and all the baby Carolines will live happily ever after.'

He lay back, delighted with the beauty of it all.

'No,' said Ned.

'Why not?' asked Professor Muffet, irritated.

'There are limits,' said Ned.

Professor Muffet became irritated. He was

getting cold and he thought that Ned Hump was being very ungracious. He and the other historians had tried very hard to give Ned a high mark. But the essay on the Early Sardinian Trade Routes had been really atrocious.

It was not as if they minded Ned's disagreeing with them; but if he *did* disagree, he had to give at least one good reason. And all his reasons had been terrible. Professor Muffet remembered one or two of them, and shivered in spite of himself.

On the other hand, all Ned's other answers in the exams had been very good indeed, which was why he'd been able to persuade the others to give Ned this second chance tomorrow.

And now it looked as though Ned was going to throw this second chance away. He was just being stubborn and ungrateful, and was acting as though everybody in the world was against him.

If it hadn't been for the after-effects of the whisky still softening him a little, Professor Muffet might have lost his temper with Ned Hump. But as it was, he just said: 'Sad. Sad to see a young man so soon upon the scrap-heap. Flung there to fester by his own stubbornness and stupidity. Sad, sad, oh Clio.'

Ned said, 'Sad. Sad to see a man of fame and

distinction suggesting to an untried but honest stripling that he should indulge in lies to get himself a job and a stubborn wife who is probably too nasty to live with for more than a week at a time anyhow.'

Professor Muffet smiled to himself. He thought that Ned and Caroline would probably fit together very well, married.

Ned was, at this moment, seized with a desire for action. He too was getting cold. He drew his knees up under and pulled in his elbows. He gathered himself on all fours. He pushed hard up at the top end and levered himself up onto his feet. He felt as though he had achieved something great.

He walked round to the other side of the sundial and held out both hands to pull the professor to his feet.

Mandy rolled out of the jacket sideways, still fast asleep.

'I ought to go home,' said Ned.

'Impossible,' said Professor Muffet. 'You must sleep here tonight. It would be churlish to throw you out so late, so far from home. You need as much sleep as you can get before tomorrow afternoon, and all the buses must have stopped hours ago.'

'Where shall I sleep?' Ned asked. 'I don't want to sound choosy, but I'm not fond of sofas. I am prone to falling off them and bruising myself rather badly. I think I must have very tender skin.'

Professor Muffet inwardly made a little face. Then he said, 'There's a small bed made up in case of emergencies such as yourself, in the attic. Behind a green door. All the doors up there are green, but this one apparently has a long and deep scratch in the paintwork, which Mrs Phipps feels I ought to do something about. Mandy went berserk there once while Aunt Alice was staying. It was Aunt Alice's fox stole, as I remember, that started all the trouble. I don't blame Mandy. Even I could smell that fox stole miles away. But you can sleep there.'

'Where?' said Ned. He was a little confused, and wondered if he was being offered a fox stole to sleep in.

'In the attic,' said Professor Muffet. 'In a bed behind a green door with a scratch. I thought I had made that quite plain.'

He woke his guide dog with a 'Hey, *Mandy*' – and a prod with his foot.

Ned tugged both of them across the lawn and back into the study. While Ned closed and locked the French windows, the professor bent down to pat his dog goodnight.

'Night night,
Sleep tight,
Mind the fleas,
And don't bite,' he told her.

Ned said, 'You look after that dog a lot better than she looks after you.'

Professor Muffet said, in hot defence of his dog, 'She rises to the occasion,' and added, out of honesty, 'On occasions.'

They parted on the landing. Professor Muffet stumbled into his own bedroom and Ned pulled himself unsteadily up the attic stairs, with the help of the banisters, in search of a green door with a long scratch.

Both of them were tired to death.

In the middle of the night, Ione was half awakened by what seemed to be a series of thumps on the ceiling above her. Her mind was thick with dreaming. She rolled over, thinking vaguely that Caroline must have fallen out of the narrow bed in the attic. But since she had warned Caroline before they parted, and Caroline had been so very forthright about her own slimness, Ione didn't feel in the least responsible. She rolled over and drifted back, deeper, into her dream.

Soon after he'd fallen asleep, Professor Muffet was half awakened by what seemed to be a series of thumps on the floor of the attic. His mind was thick with the after-effects of whisky, and with dreaming. He rolled over, thinking vaguely that Ned must be prone to falling out of beds as well as off sofas. But there was nothing he could do about Ned's sense of balance, or his tender skin, so he did not feel in the least responsible. He rolled over and drifted back, deeper, into his dream.

In the middle of the night, Caroline was half awakened by a cold pressure on her bare shoulder. She rolled over in the narrow attic bed, her mind thick with dreaming. She thought, vaguely, that Mandy must have forced the door and be nuzzling up against her. But Caroline decided that she was in no way responsible for Mandy's nocturnal wanderings. She rolled over and tried to drift back, deeper, into her dream.

But the coldness came again, on the same shoulder as before.

'Move over,' a voice said. 'Move over. Stop hogging. Move *over*.'

Caroline woke with a start.

She sat bolt upright, clutching the sheet to her bare body.

Ned Hump, dressed in a pair of mauve underpants, a string vest and odd socks, was trying to get into her bed.

Caroline stared. Then she attacked.

'Get out of here *at once*, Ned Hump,' she flared. 'Get *straight* out of my bed and then *straight* out of my room.'

Ned Hump continued trying to shift her over with his elbow.

'Move *over*,' he persisted. He was cold. It had taken him ages to find the green door, and the scratch, and then ages longer to get partly undressed. He was getting colder every moment.

'Move *over*,' he insisted. 'Stop *hogging. I've* been given this bed for the night, you know. So stop hogging and move over, and then perhaps I'll let you stay.'

Caroline lost her temper.

She pushed as hard as she possibly could with one foot without losing either her dignity or her sheet.

Ned Hump fell heavily onto the uncarpeted floor.

Caroline said, 'You are the most pushy, ill-mannered, rude and boorish person in the world. Get out of my bed and my room this *instant*.'

Ned Hump hardly listened. He was tentatively fingering his right thigh. He thought he might well have bruised himself badly in the fall. Then he lost his temper, too.

He said, 'You are the most rough, selfish, hoggish and ungenerous woman in the world. Move over *this instant* and let me into that bed.'

Caroline laughed like a witch.

'You must be *mad*,' she shouted. 'Professor Muffet is dead right.' She shifted angrily against the pillows. 'You must be totally *insane* to think that I'd let you into this bed. This is my bed.'

The repetition of the word bed reminded her how tired she was. Her whole body seized up in a yawn, and she heard only the tail end of Ned's next insult: '...in the *world*!'

'What?' she said.

Ned floundered around for something even more devastating to say. Finally, he made do with, 'Just wait till we're married, Caroline Hope. I'll fix you good and proper.'

Caroline was almost asleep. Her violent outburst had exhausted her. But she rallied enough to say, 'You and I shall never, *ever* be married, Ned Hump. Never, ever, *ever.*'

From way down in the sheets and pillows, she pointed at the door. 'Get out,' she said. 'Get out, get out, get *out.*'

Ned went all cunning.

'I will leave,' he said softly, 'but only, *only* if you promise me faithfully, on your honour, that you *will* marry me; no strings, no fridges, hedges for life and all, within a fortnight.'

'And if I refuse?' The voice came weakly from the pillows.

'Then I shall leap into this bed and attack you.'

Caroline's head reeled.

This could go on all *night*, she thought to herself. This could go on till *morning. Nothing* could be worse than this. *Anything*, even fifty years of Ned, would be better than no sleep now.

She collapsed. She gave in entirely.

'I promise,' she said, and fell fast asleep. She could not even keep a grip on her senses long enough to make sure that he kept his promise and left the room.

Made temporarily ecstatic by the success of his

ploy, Ned leaned over and kissed her. How odd, he thought to himself: her hair tastes of coconut.

Then he stood up and gathered his shirt, trousers and shoes from the floor.

At the doorway, he turned back.

'I warn you,' he said. 'I warn you here and now that, if you renege, if you back down, if you cheat on me in this, then I shall take an unspeakable revenge upon you. I shall wait. For years, if necessary. I shall wait until your wedding day. The day of the wedding of Miss Caroline Hope to some nice, clean, shaven, respectable, employed Chartered Accountant. A Chartered Accountant with Notions about Roofs Over Heads, and Good Starts In Life, and Little Somethings Put Away In Case Of Rainy Days, and so on and so forth. I shall wait until you are walking, dressed from head to toe in pure white, clutching your lilies, hot-foot from some altar, down some yew-lined, shady church walk. And I shall be there, lurking behind some tombstone. And I shall shout out from behind this tombstone, I shall shout out' – he paused to think of something perfectly dreadful that he could shout out at her from behind the tombstone, but nothing sprang to mind, so he finished, a little lamely – 'I shall shout out something *perfectly dreadful*, and all the wedding guests will faint from absolute *horror* and *dismay*, and your mother-in-law will *scream* from *sheer shock*, and everyone, *everyone*, will turn and *stare* at you.'

He left the room.

Caroline, fast asleep, had not heard a single word.

Ned Hump couldn't find the light switch in the study, so he couldn't find the sofa. But he heard, from one corner, Mandy's heavy, drowsy breathing.

Ned and Mandy spent the rest of that night fast asleep together, cuddled up close and warm under the study desk, paw in hand.

Chapter 7

The first person to wake the next morning was Ione. It was just after five. The sun was pouring maliciously through her window, lighting up her headache and dazzling her sleep-befuddled brain.

She felt as though she had spent several weeks in a desert. She staggered across her bedroom to the small wash-basin in the corner, and drank four toothmugfuls of minty-tasting water, one after another. Then she felt her way back into bed, snuggled down and fell asleep again.

The second waking, soon after eight, was also Ione's. But this time she felt marvellous – no more thirst, no more headache – just the thought that it was clearly going to be an even more beautiful day than yesterday had been, and there would be four people for breakfast instead of two. There was even the hope that Caroline would still be feeling as romantic about Ned as she so obviously had been feeling for at least some of the time the evening before, and so might at long last agree to marry him.

Ione dressed at a frantic speed and flew down the stairs, into the sun-soaked hall. On the doormat lay a note, crumpled from having been pushed in a hurry through the letterbox. It was from Mrs Phipps, and written in spidery writing on the back of a gas bill. The note said:

> *Can't do for you today, dears. Mollie's baby's come, and about time too as she's larger than a bus, poor thing, so I am off up there this very moment.*

Ione thrust the note into her jeans pocket, and went through into the kitchen. Here she stood in absolute consternation, gazing at the chaos. How *could* she and Caroline have sat in all this mess for so long last night, just giggling and playing cards?

Ione set to, determinedly, to clear everything up.

In fact, the mess was not nearly so bad, or so thick or encrusted as it at first sight appeared. By half past eight, Ione had the kitchen looking almost normal. Everything that moved had been washed up, put away or thrown into the bin. Everything that didn't move had been wiped with a damp cloth.

Ione swept the floor and collected one last dustpanful of scraps, mostly coconut biscuit crumbs. She thought that perhaps she ought to mop the floor as well. She knew it was tacky because her bare feet stuck to it as she moved around, and at each step she almost had to peel her feet off the tiles. But then she decided she wouldn't bother and laid the table for breakfast instead.

She pulled another two chairs up close, and set out cereals and a toast-rack and sugar and the milk-jug and cutlery and bowls.

She decided as she worked that when each person came down, she might offer to put an egg on to boil; but that any fried-bacon eaters would have to cook their own. She thought she would not be able to bear standing over sizzling bacon with her back to everyone teasing one another and joking about all the things they had done and said and sung the night before.

When everything was ready, she stopped for a second. She could hear, from somewhere upstairs, assorted getting-up noises.

She toasted the bread and filled the teapot. When she turned round with it, only one person had come down and taken a place at the table, and that was her father. He sat in his usual seat.

Ione put down the teapot and sat in her usual seat.

'Tea?' she asked.

'Yes, please,' he said, and proffered his stripy blue mug in her direction.

It could, she thought, have been any old day at all.

Professor Muffet drank his tea in silence. He looked most glum. Ione assumed that this was partly because of the drinking the night before, and partly because he had to spend almost all of a truly beautiful day sitting in a bleak hall round a table with a lot of equally glum other historians, examining young people like Ned Hump on their knowledge of Early Sardinian Trade Routes and the like.

She thought, if she were in his position, she would feel pretty gloomy too. So she companionably kept his silence with him.

After his second piece of toast, Professor Muffet asked his daughter gravely, 'Ione, do you think Ned Hump has any sense at all?'

Ione said promptly and loyally that she thought he did.

The silence fell between them again. Ione listened for further getting-up sounds through the house, but there were none.

After his third piece of toast, Professor Muffet asked, 'Do you think there is any chance whatsoever of his behaving sensibly this afternoon?'

Ione considered. Then she said dubiously, 'I *think* that I think that there is.'

'I don't,' said the professor. 'I don't for one moment think that I think that there is.'

He stood up.

'I must go,' he said. 'Or I shall be late.' He picked up his jacket from where it hung over the back of his chair. 'Though there would be a consolation in being late,' he said. 'I would miss Paul Bisons's performance, which is bound to be abysmal.' Ione dusted off his jacket while he called Mandy.

Ione passed him Mandy's leading rein, and Professor Muffet buckled it on. At the front door, with one hand on the latch, and the other restraining Mandy, he kissed his daughter goodbye.

He looked, Ione thought, grey and tired and

very, very depressed. And as he left he said again, 'I don't for one moment think that I think there is hope. But *if* hope springs, tell Ned that there's a braille copy of Punkle's *Early Sardinian Trade Routes and Their Implications* under the lampstand in the study, and Caroline can read it to him.'

Ione's eyes followed him as he walked down the garden path, dragging his feet a little in the gravel.

She wondered why he was so very fond of Ned Hump, and so very concerned that Ned should not spoil his second chance.

For the first time ever, it occurred to Ione that her parents might have planned to have more children than just herself. They might have wanted to have a son as well – a son like Ned. The more she thought about it, the clearer it all seemed. Of *course* her father would have wanted a son; and he would have loved to have had a son like Ned.

Ione could understand that with no trouble at all, for she would have loved to have had a brother like him too.

Ione made the largest resolution of her life. She resolved to tell lies, mislead and act – all day if necessary – to get what she wanted.

And what she wanted was that Ned Hump should do as well as he possibly could in his examination that afternoon, so that her father would come home happy. She sat in the sunlight on the bottom stair and resolved solemnly and silently that not even Ned Hump was going to get the chance to spoil things for himself one single time more.

Ione sat in the sunlight on the bottom stair, and she carefully hatched her plot.

The first part of the plot involved taking Caroline her breakfast in bed.

Ione pushed down the handle with her elbow, and kicked the attic door open with her foot. She slid inside with the tray, then set it down on the bedside table with as loud a crash as she could manage without breaking anything. Caroline still didn't stir. So Ione swept the cheerful, yellow-spotted curtains apart to let the sun stream in unhampered, waking Caroline far more effectively than the kick on the door and the crash of the breakfast tray.

Caroline groaned and burrowed, but the harsh sunlight seemed to be able to attack her even through the sheet.

She surrendered to the inevitability of morning, and sat up.

Ione sat on the end of the bed, on the tattered old patchwork quilt which had been stitched together by Aunt Alice when Uncle Arthur was off at some war, and was now coming apart again.

'Morning,' said Ione in her simple voice. 'Lovely morning. Daddy's gone. Ned's still fast asleep. I'm up, though.'

'So I see,' said Caroline in her acid voice.

She peered at the tray and groped for the teacup. 'Is that really *toast*?' she asked, prodding a square soggy lump that lay as though dying on the plate. 'It looks centuries old.'

Ione thought privately that, had her plot not been at risk, she could have banged the entire tray over Caroline's head. She would not have been scalded. The tea was quite cold too. But Ione held her tongue.

'The tea is quite cold too,' said Caroline.

Ione pulled threads out of the quilt. She would have preferred to broach the subject gently, or let it arise naturally out of the conversation. But it didn't look as if there was going to *be* much conversation; just a series of insults to her breakfast.

Time was, she feared, running short. Ned might get up at any moment, and disappear. There was no time for roundabout openings. She would have to charge straight in.

'Does everyone like Ned as much as Dad and I do?' she said.

'I suppose so.' Caroline leaned back on her pillows, pushing hair from her eyes. She sipped her cold tea. 'Most people do. He has one of those faces, I think.'

She was quite pointedly, Ione thought, pretending that the buttered toast no longer existed. However, sacrifices have to be made.

'And does Ned like everyone back?'

'I suppose so.' Caroline yawned. She stretched out in all directions at once. Ione decided that Caroline was really quite beautiful – all dopey and straggled though she was. Ione also decided that there was no real need to be subtle and roundabout. It was just a waste of time. Caroline was still half asleep.

'It's funny, isn't it,' said Ione bluntly, 'how some people never seem to get mean or spiteful or jealous. And Ned seems to be one of those people. I mean, suppose something horrid were to happen to him. Suppose' – she pretended to think, to come out with the example as though it were the first thing to come into her head – 'suppose somebody else, somebody he didn't like particularly, and thought was dreadful at history, was to be offered this job that is free now that Higgins is having to have a long rest. Would Ned *still* be happy and kind? Is he *really* that nice all through?'

She sat on the end of the bed and waited, casually pulling more threads out of Aunt Alice's quilt. She was hoping desperately that Caroline would take the bait quickly, and yet not notice she'd done so.

Caroline continued to sip her cold tea. 'I think Ned is fairly easy-going,' she said. 'I mean, that's one of his problems.'

Ione thought of the sundial: 'Seize the present moment; the evening hour is nigh', and the way Ned had read it out loud just after they met. He had recognized this weakness in himself too. He had *said* that was another of his problems. So really she would be helping him to be what he knew he ought to be. Lying did unnerve Ione rather, but now she felt quite cheered, and almost justified.

Caroline went on: 'I think he'd remain nice,

whoever got the job.' She shifted around in the bed. Ione was cramping her feet.

'Is this really tea, or is it coffee?' she asked. 'It tastes a little like both, but not much like either.'

'It's tea,' said Ione coldly. She was wondering whether, by furthering Ned's aims to marry Caroline, she was really doing him much of a favour. Caroline could be quite a pig when she tried, Ione thought.

As though to prove this judgement unfair, Caroline smiled warmly. 'He'd be much nicer than *I* would, anyhow,' she said generously. 'But then, he *is* much nicer than I am.' Ione did not deny this, as she felt courtesy demanded; but she warmed to Caroline again. 'And I truly think he'd just be pleased for the person who was given the job.' She giggled. 'Except, of course . . .' At the very thought, she giggled again.

'Except . . . ?' repeated Ione, breathless.

Caroline was shaking with amusement. 'Except, of course,' she said, 'if Paul Bisons, or someone like that, who's thick as two planks, and horrid with it, were to get the job. Then, even Ned would go wild.'

She looked up from her tea, expecting Ione to ask her all about Paul Bisons.

But Ione had already rushed from the room. She had the name, and she didn't need anything else. Paul Bisons, Paul Bisons, Paul Bisons. She jammed the name into her head on every step down to the kitchen.

Caroline shrugged, and finished the coffee-tasting tea. Then she snuggled back down, deliciously, into the bed.

She had no idea how very helpful she had been.

A short time after, Ned Hump emerged from the study, crumpled, grubby and bedraggled. His sleep had been interrupted by the most extraordinary noise, as of elephants cantering down stairs, he thought.

He groped his way along the hall to the kitchen, and found the sink. He splashed cold water all over his face, to waken himself completely. Then he turned back from the sink, his face drenched and droplets of water clinging to his eyelashes. His eyes looked huge in his drawn face. Although he wouldn't admit it, even to himself, Ned was chilled by the thought of the afternoon's ordeal.

Ione smiled sweetly at him, and tried to look

as though she had been sitting there, with her back straight, calmly peeling vegetables, for hours and hours. In fact, she had had only a few seconds in which to fill the bowl with water, throw in some potatoes and sit down. But Ned did not know that.

Ione sat, cool as could be, peeling her potatoes as though she had quite got into the rhythm, and smiled at him sweetly. It was a real Caroline smile. Her mind was busy mixing poison on which she planned to half-choke him.

'Sleep well?' she asked pleasantly.

'In the end,' he said, and smiled back at her. His sleep had begun with nightmares about the coming exam. It was only sheer exhaustion that had given him rest in the end.

But neither his wan look nor his friendly smile deterred Ione from her purpose. She waved a half-peeled potato towards the window, where it caught in a stream of sunlight, and said, 'Lovely day. It's already getting hot.'

'It is,' he said. 'And you shouldn't be stuck in here, peeling spuds. You should be out lazing on a lawn, chewing daisies and counting butterflies.'

Ione sighed heavily.

'I *have* to stay in,' she said sadly. 'Mrs Phipps

isn't coming today. She sent a note saying Mollie's baby is on the way, and she's had to rush up there to help. So I have to do all the cooking.' She sighed again, even more heavily than before.

'You don't,' said Ned.

He sat opposite and, tugging a lump of bread off the crusty end of the loaf, began to chew his way through it.

'You don't have to cook at all. It's far too hot. Just wait till everyone is starving and they don't mind *what* they eat, then uproot a lettuce and rush in here for two seconds to open a couple of tins of something. Then go straight outside again.'

Ione said pathetically, 'It isn't lunch that I have to prepare. It's a proper dinner. For tonight. For a guest. Three courses, and wine, and all that.'

Ned ripped off another lump of bread.

'Who has your father invited for dinner?' he asked, as she had planned he would.

'I don't know yet,' said Ione. 'It hasn't been decided.'

She waited for him to question this curious statement, but he didn't. For the first time Ione saw drawbacks in tact like Ned's, so to prompt him she added, 'I just wish I knew if he's a big potato eater, whoever he is. It's so difficult to know how many to peel otherwise.'

Ned reached out for a banana. 'It's a he, then, is it?' he said, and added helpfully, 'Usually, you can tell from the person's size. What size are all these men who might, or might not, be invited for dinner?'

Ione carried the bowl of potato peelings around to the sink behind Ned, and poured the water out. 'It's only a decision between two,' she said. She kept her back to him as the water drained away. She always felt safer, lying, when she had her back to the person to whom she was telling the lies.

This is it, she thought to herself. This is it.

'I don't know the size of the other person it could be,' she said slowly. 'I mean, it could be *you* who is invited, in which case I will need to peel lots more.' She paused. 'Or it could be a person called Paul Bisons.' She paused again, in order to let the name float around the room a little, and not get lost in her sentence. 'In which case I may already have peeled far too many.'

'Why,' said Ned, equally slowly, as he rose to take the bait, 'why should your father choose to invite either Paul Bisons or myself to dinner with him tonight?' Unthinkingly, he placed the banana he had been chewing back on the pile of fruit in the bowl, peeled and half eaten. 'And when,' he continued dangerously, 'am I to know if *I* am the lucky man? Alternatively, when am I to know if Paul Bisons is to be the man who is going to pig all those spuds?'

He finished his questions with real venom in his voice. Ione sang an inward hymn of praise to Caroline for picking what was so clearly *just* the right name.

'I suppose,' said Ione, pretending to fish in the plughole for small peelings that had got away, but concentrating hard on her lying instead. 'I suppose you will know after your exam this afternoon. You see, Dad says he ought to invite the man who is asked to take over Higgins's job to dinner tonight. He says it's the custom to invite a new historian to dinner.'

She waited for the explosion.

And it came.

'Paul Bisons?' repeated Ned. 'Paul *Bisons*? The new *historian*? *Paid* to do something he can no more do than sing soprano? Given a *room* in the university in which to write the drivel *he* writes? I can hardly *believe* it.'

Ione plopped all the icing on her lie in one go.

'Dad says he's very good indeed on the Early Sardinian Trade Routes,' she said.

Ned rose to his feet. He was breathing fast. His face went scarlet with rage.

'I think,' he said, raising his voice, 'I think that your father must have gone just a little *off his head* about these Early Sardinian Trade Routes of his. It seems to be reaching the stage where, if anybody dares to disagree with him about them, that's curtains for them.'

Ione said nothing. She just waited.

'I think,' continued Ned Hump, shouting now, 'I think that your father is beginning to act a little like *God*, telling everyone what to believe and what not to believe. And only a deity or a fool would wish to invite a brainless cretin like Paul Bisons to take a job within a *thousand miles* of himself, let alone in the same damn *building*. I think that Paul Bisons is the most—'

That was when her head hit him in the stomach, full-square.

'*Ouch!*' he howled, driven backwards onto the floor, clutching his belly in a great spasm of pain. For Ione had started her own explosion now. And when Ione decided to explode, she could explode louder and further and better than *ever* Ned Hump could.

She had charged, head lowered, the entire length of the kitchen, and butted Ned in the stomach at full speed. The potato peeler, which she had left in her hand by mistake, had grazed Ned's wrist and drawn blood, adding a touch of verisimilitude to the performance that Ione would not have dared to aspire to with forethought.

And while Ned sat, winded, on the kitchen floor, clutching his stomach with one hand, and sucking blood off the other wrist, Ione ranted at him.

She went wild.

'That's *not fair*,' she shrieked. 'That's not fair *at all*. That's just *so unfair*! You're *crazy*, that's your problem. You think that just because you disagree with my father, then you're going to do badly in this exam. Well, you're *wrong*, and a *pig*, and *ungrateful* and *stubborn* and *stupid*! Because Dad says you don't have to have the same views as he does, and all the other historians have, *at all*. You just have to be able to give one single tiny *reason* for any view you want to hold. And Dad says you *can't*. He says he's been listening to you *all term*, and your reasons are *crummy*. And after they read your essay on the Early Sardinian Trade Routes in the exam last month, all the other historians said it was absolutely atrocious, and a *rabbit* couldn't hold views like that without blushing for shame.'

She took a deep breath. Ned was staring at her.

More icing, she thought. More icing.

'So they said to give you one mark, and my father said *No*. It was my dad who insisted that you had this second chance. He said you might come to your senses. He told them you were having a little brainstorm from the strain of the exams. He said you were really clever, and couldn't truly believe a word of what you wrote in that dreadful essay. He said you'd act sensibly and think again, and then you might get a really good degree. Because you were only a few marks away, and if it wasn't for that stupid, *stupid* essay, you would have got a really good degree *anyway*.'

Ned Hump stared at her – a little tornado of concern, with almost-real tears in her eyes and a voice that was cracking at the edges. He thought he had never seen anyone lose control so badly.

Ione stared towards Ned Hump. She could not see his face too clearly because of the tears; but she could see him well enough.

More icing, she thought. More icing.

'But my father's sick and tired of fighting for you, Ned Hump,' she shouted. 'He says so, and it's true. It shows, too. Just before he left here this morning, when you hadn't even got *up*, he was busy trying to find a copy of Punkle's *Early Sardinian Trade Routes and Their Implications*, just in case, *just in case* you decided to act like a sane person for once. He didn't even have time to have any *breakfast* before he left, he was looking so hard. He's probably *starving* now.'

Even Ione felt a little guilty about this part of her speech, but she was too far in now to back down. So she went on.

'He's *always* been fond of you, Ned Hump, you stupid, *stupid* idiot, ever since he began to teach you.'

She broke off, just to keep her head still for a second, so he would be sure to see the tears, before they dried off.

'That's why he calls you a loon,' she went on when she was sure he had noticed them. 'That's why he calls you the *loon.*' She brushed her fringe out of her eyes so she could see his face properly.

'When I was very young,' she said, her voice

soft and quiet now, 'when I was very, very little, he used to call *me* his loon.'

That was enough. That was all the icing there was.

Ione stood in the middle of the kitchen and watched, through tear-dampened lashes, as Ned Hump turned ashen-pale.

She watched him thinking, and she knew exactly what he thought. And only when, at last, he climbed to his feet and left the room without a word, did she let her body go limp.

She dropped onto a chair and stared into space.

It had been, without a shadow of a doubt, the best performance of her entire life.

From beginning to end, it had been *magnificent*.

A few minutes later, Ned Hump came back into the kitchen. He had stuck an enormous sticking plaster onto his wrist. It was as wide as the scratch was long.

'Where's that Punkle book?' he demanded, with a red face. 'Where *is* it?'

'Daddy put it under the lampstand in the study for you,' said Ione. 'But it's in braille.'

Ned looked taken aback. Then his face went firm again.

'Go and wake Caroline,' he told her. '*She* can read it to me. Go and wake Caroline.'

Ned went off again to find the Punkle book, muttering something about Paul Bisons under his breath.

Ione went and woke Caroline.

Chapter 8

After such a tempestuous start, the rest of that morning seemed strangely quiet and peaceful to Ione.

Ned and Caroline sat together on the bottom veranda step, in the shade from the open French windows. Caroline was reading out, in her soft, chokey voice, all the important bits of the Punkle book, running her fingertips over the braille as fast as she possibly could.

Ned had his arm around her. As she reached the end of each section, he would nuzzle her ears like a friendly horse after sugar lumps. He wanted more than anything to hold her hand; but that would have slowed up her reading impossibly.

In between the nuzzlings, he was concentrating hard. Read aloud by Caroline, Punkle's views on the Early Sardinian Trade Routes sounded quite sensible. Infinitely more sensible than Ned had ever found them before.

Ione had forsaken her bowl of potatoes and peelings. She put the ones that had been fully peeled into a saucepan of salted water, and the ones she had only half peeled or hadn't yet started on back in the vegetable rack in the larder. She hoped they would dry off without going mouldy first.

There was only one more part of her plot. This was the easiest part of all, and quite the most pleasant. All the big lies were over now.

Ione crept upstairs for her sandals, and then slid as quietly as she could out of the back door, and up the hill to Mollie's house. She wanted to find Mrs Phipps. She needed advice.

She told Mrs Phipps that she wanted to make a splendid, different, surprise, end-of-examination, going-to-get-married celebration tea for everybody, and make no noise at all while she was doing it so that no one would guess until the very last moment what she was about.

What should she do?

Mrs Phipps was, at the moment Ione arrived, flustered half to death. She tried to think, but thinking was almost impossible. Mollie's baby was making itself felt in more and more regular bursts, yet Mollie herself was insisting on finishing her game of Scrabble with her husband, Ted. Mrs Phipps kept telling Mollie that the game could be finished just as easily at the hospital, but Mollie swore that Ted was not to be trusted for a moment with her pile of letters, and had so far refused to budge.

Mrs Phipps tried to think of the simplest solution – and the quickest to explain to Ione.

'Take all the housekeeping money out of the pudding basin on the third shelf of the larder and go down to Waley's in the village and buy two large tubs of double cream and all the strawberries they have in the shop. And don't you let him sell you cream on the turn, just because you're young. You check the date stamp.'

Hearing the sound of a scuffle behind her, Mrs Phipps speeded up. She spoke so fast, Ione could barely keep up. 'Whip up the cream a bit with the squiggly tin thing – you'll find that in the spoon drawer – not too much now, not stiff. And take the stumps off all the strawberries and put them in a colander ready to rinse them. And at the very last minute, you do that and cut them in half lengthways because they go further that way, and serve them with cream on top in blobs in those knobbly glass dishes. Some people might need sugar. Use caster sugar.'

'Won't two large tubs of double cream and all the strawberries in Waley's be an awful lot?' Ione asked. After all, they would only be four for tea.

But Mrs Phipps had assumed that, with all Ione had listed to be celebrated, there must be at least a dozen people coming. 'It'll be just right,' she assured her.

Relieved, Ione rushed down the path. Just as she reached the gate, Mrs Phipps called to her again.

'If it's *really* special,' she said. 'Go down the cellar, and mind all those dreadful rotten steps or you'll fall and hurt yourself, and get out some of the white wine, and bung that in the fridge, too, to keep cool.'

'Wine?' said Ione. She thought she really had started something.

Mollie yelled then, good and loud and long. In fact, it was because she had just looked up potato in the dictionary, and it didn't have an e on the end, but Mrs Phipps did not know that, and she hastily waved Ione out of the garden.

* * *

Ione ambled through her errands. It was getting hotter, fast.

She found the housekeeping money in the pudding basin, though it wasn't on the third shelf at all, unless you were counting upwards from the floor, which was, Ione thought, daft. She walked down to Waley's, and bought the cream and the strawberries.

She whipped up the cream with the squiggly tin thing, not too much, and put it in the fridge. Then she took the stumps off the strawberries and put them in a colander, ready to rinse.

After that, she washed all the knobbly glass bowls and all the small spoons.

Lastly, she opened the cellar door and peered down into the dark. It was here that her courage failed her completely, for there was no light in the cellar.

She wondered if she dared interrupt Ned and Caroline's working, to ask for their help. She crept along the hall and into the study, and peered out through the French windows.

The Punkle book was lying forgotten on the lawn, its edges curling upwards in the sun's heat, and Ned and Caroline were kissing.

Ione walked outside.

'Ned, Caroline,' she said, after a polite little cough, 'are you afraid of cobwebs and spiders and the dark and all that?'

Caroline spoke first.

'I bet Ned's scared of spiders,' she said. 'It's more than likely. He's scared of me, and I only have *two* arms.'

She attacked Ned with her two arms, and they fell together off the bottom step and onto the lawn.

Ione waited patiently for them to unravel. Then she said, 'Would one of you please go down into the cellar for me?'

Ned shook some blades of grass and his wife-to-be off his shoulders, and said, 'Just show me the way,' chivalrously to Ione.

Ione showed him the cellar door and lit him a candle. Ned stepped down two of the creaking, planky steps into the gloom.

'Before the darkness swallows me entirely,' he said, 'perhaps never to yield up my body again, would you be so good as to tell me what you are sending me down here for?' He held out his plastered wrist for her to feel guilty. 'Or is it merely attempted murder, like this morning?'

Ione giggled.

'Wine,' she told him. 'White wine.'

'Wine,' he repeated. 'White wine.' He looked up at her sternly. 'What *sort* of white wine?'

She considered. Her secret was at risk. And since she had been lying to him all morning, one more little one couldn't matter much.

So she said, 'I'm not sure. I've forgotten what it's called. But I remember that it's the same sort as we had one day when we had strawberries and cream at Aunt Alice's house.'

Ione really was a superb liar, when she put her mind to it.

'Good clue,' said Ned, and disappeared, apart from a few mild flickerings of his candle, into the cellar deeps.

Ione waited on tenterhooks at the top of the steps. A short while later, Ned sent up a loud and echoing shout. 'How many bottles?'

Ione counted up people. Four people, with luck, for it did seem as if Caroline was going to stay all day.

'Eight,' she said.

'*Eight?*'

'Eight.'

'Eight.'

At that moment, Ned was attacked by a

ferocious spider, and so was distracted from asking more questions. He brought up the bottles in two journeys, and Ione stacked them, lying on their sides, in the fridge. She kept the fridge door half shut, as she did so, so that Ned could not see the strawberries or the cream that were already inside.

Before putting the last bottle in, she looked at its label.

'It doesn't *say* it's good with strawberries,' she said suspiciously.

Ned Hump leaned against the table and took another banana from the fruit bowl. He seemed to be addicted to bananas.

'One great long mystery, wine,' he informed her. 'That is why I stick to cider. It's cheaper, and you know where you are.'

He added over his shoulder as he returned to Caroline, 'Also, you can keep cider in sensible places, like under your bed. You don't feel obliged to keep it in a dark cellar where, in their turn, belligerent spiders feel obliged to attack you each time you feel like a quick swig.'

His voice trailed away.

Ione giggled and went off to the study, to find some glasses. Judging by the smears all over the

111

knobbly bowls, the glasses would probably need washing too, she thought. Mrs Phipps obviously had her blind spots as daily help.

Just before two, Ned came back into the kitchen. He looked quite smart.

'I have stolen one of your father's shirts for the day,' he said. 'And a tie. This shirt must be far too large for him, since it almost fits me.' He ran a finger around the back of his neck, to loosen it a little. 'Almost,' he repeated, uneasily.

'And now I've come to ask if I can make myself a sandwich. Since I appear to be living here at present, it seems only fair that I should be fed.'

Ione found him some rolls to fill with large slabs of cheese. She knew cheese was nourishing. As fast as he could fill the rolls, Ned ate them, taking all the while between mouthfuls.

'I'm leaving this house now,' he told her. 'I have listened to as much of Punkle's *Early Sardinian Trade Routes and Their Implications* as I can stomach, and now I am going to go for a very long walk to clear my head. Kindly keep my wife-to-be from following me. She's very distracting.'

'Is Caroline really going to marry you?' asked Ione. 'Really and truly?'

'I think I have beaten her into submission,' said Ned complacently. 'I think she has bored herself into weakness with all those refusals. I think the worm has, at long last, turned.'

He waved his roll at her.

'I shan't come back here between my walk and the exam,' he said. 'So whether or not I return to this house will depend on how it goes. If it goes badly, I shall take drastic action, and you'll find my body bleeding gently in some nearby ditch.' He took another mouthful. 'In the interests of historical studies,' he added, 'I shall leave a trail of evidence to convince the police that I was, in fact, murdered by Paul Bisons. I trust you will employ your time, after the initial bout of grief, getting up petitions to send to the Home Secretary for the re-introduction of the death penalty.' He looked at her face. It was a little blank. 'Hanging,' he said. 'Hanging.'

She grinned.

'And if it all goes all right?' she said.

'In that case, I shall return soon after six o'clock with your father, a broad smile, a flagon of cider in my arms and a small golden ring in my pocket for my beloved to wear as soon as she can be organized into a Registry Office, or something.'

'The shops close at half past five,' warned Ione.

Ned left, clutching three more cheese rolls and another banana.

Soon after, Ione drifted out into the garden. The sun was high, and very powerful. Even the grass looked weak from the heat.

Caroline was lying on her stomach on the lawn, picking petals off a daisy.

'He loves me, he loves me not, he loves me, he loves me not, he loves me, he loves me not,' she was singing softly to herself.

'Of *course* he loves you,' said Ione, as she sat down beside her. 'That's why he came here yesterday. That's why he was trespassing in our summerhouse in the first place. That's why he's so thin, from not eating enough for worrying you'd never marry him. That's why I invited him in, and gave him all the chocolate fudge cake.'

Caroline picked another daisy. 'He'll do well this afternoon, he won't do well, he'll do well, he won't do well,' she sang instead, shredding this daisy, too.

'Of *course* he'll do well,' said Ione. '*You* know he will; *I* know he will; *Dad* knows he will; even *Ned* knows he will, now. Dad says he's one of the brightest young men he's ever taught.'

Caroline rooted around for another daisy. She had to stretch to get at it. All her hair fell in her eyes. The sun caught it, and shone spangles.

She began ripping this daisy apart. 'He'll get a job, he won't get a job, he'll get a job, he won't get a job,' she sang, petal by shredded petal.

'Of *course* he'll get a job,' said Ione. 'Dad says they need someone else to take over from poor old Higgins while he has his rest. And Ned will be very good at teaching, so they'll probably keep him on, even after Higgins comes back. Ned's a really good teacher. He's taught me a lot.'

Caroline rolled over onto her back, and shut her eyes against the harsh, half-past-two sun.

'Ione,' she said, 'I only hope that there is another man in the world as nice as Ned Hump, for you to fall in love with some day.'

Ione thought this was a lovely thing to say. She swallowed hard. She thought that Caroline was so very different now, and yet not really different at all. It was just that this gentle, not-so-irritable side of her had never really showed up much before.

It occurred to Ione that always, in the beginning, she had seen Caroline when she was being Miss Hope, always working or pouring out tea, in her efficient mood.

And then, when she had seen her with Ned, Caroline had probably been irritable because she loved him so much and was worried about him and his future. After all, even Ione's father got irritable with Ned Hump a good deal of the time, and he wasn't planning on marrying him.

She thought that Caroline was probably really nice all through, like Ned. And she was glad about that. Ione wanted the very best for Ned. She had done ever since she had first met him.

Ever since. Ever since? It was only yesterday, and not even, yet, the same time as yesterday.

At this time yesterday, she hadn't even *met* Ned Hump. She could hardly believe it. She'd met him just as the sun sank into the hedge, if you were sitting on the summerhouse floor. Not quite a whole day ago. And yet she felt as if she had known Ned Hump for years and years and years.

She felt full up, and sad, and as though, if something didn't happen quickly, she would burst into tears.

But something did happen.

Mrs Phipps's sister popped her head over the hedge and called out, 'Mollie's had a little *girl*, and now she and Ted are squabbling about what to call it, I mean her, and . . .'

Her voice was whisked away as she hurried on.

Ione lay back again. She rubbed the sadness tears back into her eyes.

'How lovely for Mollie,' she said.

Beside her, Caroline smiled at the sun, eyes tightly closed.

'How lovely for *me*,' she said softly. 'And once, when he met your mother, how lovely for your father. And soon, not long from now, how lovely for *you*.'

Ione smiled up at the sun too, red and yellow through her closed eyelids. And warm, safe and warm.

'How lovely for me,' she repeated. 'Soon, not long from now, how lovely for *me*.'

Chapter 9

All that afternoon they lay, Caroline and Ione, dead to the world, lulled by the sun's warmth, sleeping.

From time to time, Caroline would giggle softly inside her dream. Sometimes, Ione's fingertips would scrabble against the turf, unknowingly.

They slept side by side on the yellowing grass as though they might never, ever wake.

But they were awakened, in the end, by Mandy.

Just before six, she bounded across the daisies, released from her leading rein at the garden gate by Professor Muffet. She flew over the lawn, placed two rude and heavy paws on Caroline's stomach, and reached over to lick Ione's ear.

Both of them sat up, blinking against the sun and the sleep and the drowsiness of the whole afternoon. From the wickerwork gate in the hedge came the sound of voices, and a small procession of about a dozen people began to straggle untidily into the garden, droning on about this and that, the voices getting clearer and clearer over the sound of Mandy's friendly snuffles.

'Look,' said Ione. 'People.'

'Lots,' agreed Caroline. 'They must be all the historians, come back for a cup of tea.' She sat up suddenly as she realized what this meant. 'Can you see Ned?' she demanded anxiously. 'Is he there? Is he with them? Can you *see* him?'

Ione could. He was somewhere towards the back of the straggle, not yet through the gate. He was staggering under the weight of an enormous glass flagon of cider. His teeth were bared in a horrific grin, and from between his clenched teeth there was suspended a brown paper bag.

Spotting them, he speeded up to overtake the others, who were much too deep in their conversations to notice even his frantic elbowings and shoves. He finally made his way through, and over the grass to them. He towered above Caroline, clutching the cider flagon to Professor Muffet's shirt. He opened his mouth, and the brown paper bag, soggy with toothmarks, fell into Caroline's lap.

'Take it,' he told her. 'It's for you.'

She peered into the bag and up-ended it. Into her palm dropped a brass curtain ring. It glistened as bravely as it could, only being brass, in the sunlight.

'Oh, Ned,' said Caroline. 'It's lovely.' And she burst into tears.

She slipped the curtain ring onto her wedding finger. Far too large, it fell off again at once.

'Never mind,' she said, licking the tears of happiness off her flushed cheeks. 'Doesn't matter.' She stuck the curtain ring firmly and proudly onto her thumb. It fitted perfectly. 'I *love* thumb rings,' she said.

'I think you'll have to,' said Ned. 'They'd never alter it. It only cost a few pence. I had to buy five in a packet. I threw the other four away. It's not a real ring, you see. I did so want to get you a real, gold, people's ring,' he added wistfully. 'But all the proper jewellery shops were closed.'

His eyes *dared* Ione to tell him she had told him so. So she didn't.

'Only one little hardware shop would let me in to buy anything,' he went on, in explanation. 'And only then because there was someone in there, stock-taking, and I banged on the door so loudly and so long.'

'Never mind,' said Caroline again. 'Doesn't matter. I *love* thumb rings.'

She gazed up at him with the look of moon-struck adoration that Ione had so often seen Ned use on her when she was looking the other way.

Ione decided it was time to be tactful again. So she slid away, leaving them together, and threaded her way through the historians and the conversations, in search of her father.

She found him by the shrubbery, talking to an incredibly old man with hands gnarled like tree roots. He wore a hearing aid, spectacles and a large white tropical sun hat.

'Ione,' said Professor Muffet to his daughter, 'I would like you to meet the Emeritus Professor of Ancient History.' Then he bent down and whispered in her ear. 'Emeritus means retired. And he's deaf, so you have to shout.' Then he shouted, 'Bill, meet my daughter, Ione.'

Ione wondered if she ought to curtsey. He looked so unbelievably old, he might even be expecting it of her.

The Emeritus Professor of Ancient History peered at Ione.

'Spitting image of her mother,' he said, after a lengthy inspection. 'Same eyes. Lovely eyes. *Always* liked Doris's eyes,' he added wistfully.

Ione's father looked pleased. Ione, unaccountably, felt pleased, too. She had never before particularly wanted to look like her mother. All the photos of Doris Muffet made her out to be a bit of a frump. But Ione quite liked the idea of sharing her mother's eyes.

To cover her embarrassment at the compliment, she asked, 'Did Ned get all his answers right?'

Her father winced at the question. 'It isn't quite as *simple* as that, at Ned's stage,' he began to explain. But Ione could not wait till the end of an explanation, so she turned to the Emeritus Professor of Ancient History. 'Did he?' she asked him. 'Did Ned get his answers right?'

'Wouldn't know,' came the reply. 'Wasn't there. I only met everybody outside the hardware shop during the smash-and-grab, as we thought at the time. Thought I'd come along for a spot of tea, if there *is* any . . .' he said, looking around hopefully.

In desperation, Ione caught the arm of a perfect stranger. 'Please tell me,' she said, 'how Ned Hump did.'

The woman said, without even thinking Ione's question odd, 'A splendid performance, really splendid. Especially considering that earlier essay. Couldn't have done better myself on the Early Sardinian Trade Routes, and I've been into them quite deeply, you know.'

The woman turned back, and took up her former conversation.

Professor Muffet laid an arm on his daughter's shoulder.

'There's no need to *fret*,' he told her. 'Everything worked out beautifully. We practically offered him the job on the spot, except, of course, that that would never have done and we had to wait till afterwards.'

'Did he say yes?'

'Of course he said yes,' said Professor Muffet. 'It would have been most churlish of him not to, after all my efforts.'

Ione smiled to herself. And mine, she thought. And mine.

Professor Muffet had turned back to the Emeritus Professor of Ancient History. 'We had a few doubts about Hump at one time, you know,' he said. 'He was acting most strangely.'

'Like outside the hardware shop?' asked the

Emeritus Professor of Ancient History with interest, still half believing that Ned had been forcibly restrained from an all-out smash-and-grab.

'Not exactly,' said Ione's father. 'But he's quite well now, thank God. And it's only a fill-in job, till Higgins has had his long rest – that's why we didn't have to advertise – so if he goes odd again . . .' There was no threat in his voice though. He didn't believe Ned would.

'And if he doesn't go odd, can you keep him on after Higgins gets back?' asked Ione.

Professor Muffet hummed and ha'ed and we'll see'd; but she could tell he meant 'probably yes' and 'I hope so'.

'So glad,' said the Emeritus Professor of Ancient History. 'Though of course, he's not my period, and anyhow, I'm retired. But he seems a nice lad. Apart from his turns.' He looked round as if to assure himself that Ned was not in the immediate vicinity, and said to Ione, 'He says some very strange things, you know. I asked him, outside the hardware shop, how he hurt his wrist. I thought his answer might be important evidence against him when he came to trial. I think he probably cut it in some other smash-and-grab attack, earlier in the day. Can you imagine what he said? He said that a young lady had tried to peel him to death.'

He scratched his off-white hair, under his bright, white sun hat. 'Odd thing to say, don't you think?' he said. 'Seems a nice lad, though.' He scratched his head again, and turned to Professor Muffet. 'You'll have to watch this passion of his for cider,' he warned him. 'That sort of thing can break up a lot of good research. Is he a Somerset lad, do you think?'

His eyes strayed round in search of Ned, to see if he looked like a Somerset lad; but something in the shrubbery caught his attention instead. He stayed only long enough to add, 'And a bit of an embarrassment outside that shop, don't you think? After all, they were closed. I don't believe the curtain-ring tale for one moment, myself. After all, he threw them all away a little way, down the street.'

He ambled off towards the shrubbery. 'Seems a nice lad, though,' he let fall charitably, over his shoulder.

Ione stopped jumping around.

'Dad,' she said. 'Mollie has had a baby girl, and I have surprises in the fridge.'

Ione's father smiled to himself. He had met Mr

Waley walking past as he came through the gate, and Mr Waley was incapable of keeping a secret. But Ione's father could take a secret to the grave with him, so he did not tell Ione that Mr Waley had mentioned what his daughter had bought at the shop that day. Professor Muffet said only, 'Secrets in the fridge? How splendid. And a baby girl? How wonderful. But what I would have liked *most* in the world, on an afternoon like this one, is . . .' He paused, interminably. 'Let me think. What I would have liked most in the world on an afternoon like this one is strawberries and cream.'

'And a glass of white wine?' asked Ione, as casual as she could be in her excitement.

'Why, yes,' said Professor Muffet, astounded, and not for the first time either, by his daughter. 'A glass of white wine would have been just the thing.'

As Ione sped away, he said to the Emeritus Professor of Ancient History, 'You're right, Bill. She *is* the spitting image of her mother.'

But since the Emeritus Professor of Ancient History was already deep in the thickest part of the shrubbery, his comment fell on no ears at all, let alone deaf ones.

* * *

Ned steered Caroline out of the flock of muttering historians and led her to a patch of quiet on the edge of the lawn. He took her hands in his. 'Have you time,' he asked her, 'for a very quick wedding on Saturday morning?'

In answer, she kissed him. Not for the first time that day, but certainly for the longest.

In the kitchen, Ione was desperately slicing strawberries in half lengthwise to make them go further, and dropping them into the knobbly glass bowls. She spooned cream on top in thick splodges, and wedged a spoon down the side of each bowl. She forgot the caster sugar entirely in her impatience.

She rushed out with the first trayful onto the lawn, to offer bowls to all the nearest people. Then she spotted Ned.

'Ned,' she cried. '*Ned!* The *bottles!*'

Ned rose to the occasion like a well-trained butler. He stopped kissing Caroline at once, and ran for the kitchen, where he dug a corkscrew from the spoon drawer, and pulled the bottles, one after another, from the fridge.

Ione rushed in after him.

'Tea-towel,' said Ned.

She passed him one.

'Glasses,' he ordered.

She held them up, one by one, as he filled them almost to the brim.

'Tray,' he said.

She set as many as she could on the tray.

'Move,' he told her. 'Mingle and give. Return at once.'

She moved as fast as she could without spilling a drop of wine.

'And send in Caroline,' Ned shouted after her. 'It's about time she was some use. She can go round with a couple of these bottles and fill up people's glasses.'

Then he leaned against the fridge, and wondered how on earth Ione had *known* he would be offered a job, and they would all come back for tea, and strawberries and cream in such vast quantities would be called for, and as many as eight bottles might be drunk.

He never did find out that the answer was simple. On her tenterhooks that morning when she tried to work out the number of bottles Ned should bring up from the cellar, Ione had multiplied people by two, instead of dividing.

* * *

Ione stood with the last two bowls of strawberries on the edge of the shrubbery. Everyone in sight was already eating, or had already refused, a bowl-ful. To whom should she offer the only two second helpings?

Just then, the Emeritus Professor of Ancient History battered his way like a large jungle beast out of the shrubbery. Bits of twig stuck to his clothing, and his hat was awry.

Ione handed him one of the bowls. As he peered down to see what it was, his eyes lit up.

'Just the thing,' he said appreciatively. 'Just the very thing.' He squeezed her free hand with his free hand. '*Just* like your mother, you are, dear,' he said. '*Just* like her.'

Ione walked away on air and ate every last one of the strawberries in the last bowl without a trace of guilt.

Everybody became more and more happy and friendly. When the wine ran out, some people stopped drinking altogether, and some shared Ned's cider.

Ione thought everyone was wonderful. People who spoke to *her* first said something kind or flattering; and everyone *she* spoke to first interrupted her to tell her how much they were enjoying themselves, or how good the strawberries had been.

Ione worked her way around the guests to her father again.

'You're marvellous,' he told her. 'You're wonderful.' He was feeling rather euphoric.

'What shall we do,' she asked him, 'when Caroline has married Ned, and they've gone away on honeymoon?' She twisted her fingers in guilt. 'My braille reading is still so *slow*.'

Professor Muffet tried to think sensibly.

'We shall have to phone the agency,' he decided, 'and ask them to send me another Caroline for a couple of weeks. When do you suppose that she and Ned will marry?'

'Tomorrow, I should think,' said Ione. 'From the way they've been carrying on today.'

'Oh, my dear me,' said Professor Muffet. 'How long do you think they'll be away?'

Ione considered. 'I expect that they'll plan to go away for two weeks, and then they'll take another week on top of that to organize themselves back home again. Ned is that sort anyway, and Caroline seems to have lost her efficient mood altogether.'

'Three weeks,' mused her father. 'Three whole

weeks.' Then he beamed. 'Three weeks,' he said elatedly. '*Three whole weeks.*'

'So?' said Ione.

'Don't you see?' he cried, amazed that she didn't. 'Don't you *see*? Three whole *weeks*. It's almost the best excuse in the world to pack up shop for a while.'

'Pack up shop?'

'Take a holiday ourselves.'

'A *holiday*? You and *me*?'

'And Mandy, of course.'

'A *real* holiday? Away from here? Me too? At the *sea*?' Ione was beside herself.

'At the sea, if you like. Anywhere. I don't mind. Not fussy at all, as long as we're miles from Aunt Alice.' He beamed again. 'Haven't had a holiday for *ages*, have we? Not for ages and ages.'

Ione hugged herself. Then she hugged him. Then they went back onto the lawn, to the remains of their dwindling party, hand in hand. Ione was so excited that she let her father tread on an empty strawberry bowl that someone had left on the grass, near the sundial. It broke with a crunch under his foot.

'Was it a knobbly one?' asked Professor Muffet. 'I never did care for those knobbly ones.'

The Emeritus Professor of Ancient History bore down upon them. 'I say,' he said. 'Splendid *hamamelis mollis* you've got there, in the shrubbery, near that egg-cosy thing. Mind if I take a cutting back for the wife?'

'Splendid what?' asked Ione.

The Emeritus Professor of Ancient History stared at Ione. He was amazed by her ignorance. What, he asked himself, *did* they teach them nowadays? '*Hamamelis mollis*,' he repeated. 'Chinese witch-hazel. *Hamamelis mollis*.'

Ione's father made an enormous gesture, sending the large white tropical sun hat flying.

'Take the whole thing,' he said expansively. 'Uproot it. Carry it off. Take it home. We don't need it any longer. We're going to have a holiday.' He squeezed his daughter's hand tightly.

'Couldn't possibly,' said the Emeritus Professor of Ancient History. 'Far too big. Can't think what you mean.'

But his comment fell on no ears at all. Ione and her father had moved off.

Just as the sun was nearing the hedge, Ione slid off quietly to find somewhere she could be alone.

On the way across the lawn she noticed

Caroline in the study, holding the phone to her ear. Ione waved. Caroline waved back.

'I'm ringing our parents,' she called out. 'Will you and your father be free on Monday morning? *Please* say you will. We shall be getting married. They can't fit us in on Saturday.'

'Oh, yes,' said Ione. Her voice sounded almost as chokey as Caroline's. 'Oh, yes. Yes, please.'

She hurried off to the solitude of the summerhouse before she disgraced herself in front of the few remaining guests with her tears.

Chapter 10

On the summerhouse floor, yesterday's diamonds were back, just as before.

It might almost have been as though they, and Ione, had never been gone; as though nothing whatever had happened between then and now.

Ione sat cross-legged on the floor, tracing patterns with her fingertips on the cool, grey flagstones. She was thinking.

She was thinking about Caroline, and Ned, and her father, and Mandy, and Mrs Phipps, and Mollie and Ted and the baby girl, and the Emeritus Professor of Ancient History, and of all that had happened in the last twenty-four hours.

And she was thinking about the holiday that was going to happen after the wedding on Monday.

She thought, now that the sudden bout of

sobbing that had attacked her a few minutes before was quite over, that she was probably perfectly, perfectly happy.

The diamond reflections where she sat were, once again, long and elegant. Those by the far side were, once again, squat. The sun was nearly down into the hedge. The noises from the lawn died away entirely as the last guest said goodbye. And Ione sat on, in a daze, watching the last diamonds fade. It was just like yesterday.

And then she heard his voice behind her, just as before. Her heart gave such a jump that she missed hearing what he said; but she knew it was him. And she also knew that he must have seen her coming in here, and followed her from the lawn; but with his usual tact, he had waited until her crying fit was all over before he had spoken.

So she turned round to smile at him. He stood there, tall and thin, with his jacket dangling from his fingers behind his back, picking up all the dust from the doorpost that it hadn't already picked up the day before.

'*Plus ça change . . .*' he said.

'What does that mean?' she asked him.

She thought it might well be one of the very last things that she ever learned from Ned Hump, who had taught her so much; so she wanted to get it exactly right.

'It's a French proverb,' he told her. 'It means: the more things change, the more they stay the same.'

She thought about it. Then she said, 'That's not true, though. That's not true at all.'

'No,' he said. 'I never thought it was, either.'

He moved across, and dropped down in front of her. He lifted her chin with two fingers, and she forgot about the tear stains on her face.

'If it wasn't for you,' he told her, 'if it wasn't for you, I wouldn't have been able to marry Caroline, and I wouldn't have been given the job. I would have spoiled everything for myself, as usual, if it wasn't for you.'

She shook her face free, gently.

'Loon,' she said.

She knew, if he went on, she would begin to cry all over again, and harder.

'Maybe,' he said, understanding. 'But I can *thank* you, can't I?'

And he gave her a kiss on the cheek.

Then he turned and left her summerhouse, as silently as he had come into it. And he had come, as she knew, just to see her.

'Loon,' she said softly again, as the last diamond folded up into itself and faded away.

'And soon,' she comforted herself softly, 'soon, not long from now, somewhere, with someone else, how lovely for *me*.'

Interlude

After the wedding, Ione wrote down all the things she overheard during the day so she could give them as a special gift to Caroline and Ned.

'Good luck to him, that's all that I can say.'

'Rather her than me.'

'What *is* he wearing? Is that some sort of poncho?'

'Did he just pinch her bottom? Right in front of us?'

'*Squid?* At a wedding feast?'

'That's Uncle Gregory, isn't it? I thought he was in jail.'

'Has someone been *crying* on this cake?'

'I've been to some celebrations in my time, but *really . . .*'

'You would have thought the rest of us weren't even in the room.'

'Extraordinary! Quite extraordinary!'

'Bit of a scramble, the whole affair, if you want my opinion.'

'Looks more like a curtain ring to me.'

'Good luck to her, that's all that I can say.'

'They must be besotted with one another. It's the only explanation.'

'Can we go home now, please? My head is *spinning*.'

'Thank God that's over. My feet feel like mashed pulp.'

Ione's father stood and listened while she read it out to him. There was a silence, then he said to her:

'Sweetie, I hope you're not planning to give them *that*.'

Part Two

Part Two

Chapter 11

Ione sat eavesdropping on the rickety steps that led up from the parched lawn to her father's study. She had clasped her arms tightly round her bare legs, and curled over till her cheek rested against her sunburned knees. Her unbrushed hair, which the long summer's sun had bleached to the colourlessness of the dried-out grass below her, fell in a tangle, hiding her face, as if she were ashamed of sitting listening in the harsh afternoon sunlight, unseen and uninvited.

But Ione had no qualms about what she was doing. Indeed, she had shifted cautiously along the creaking boards and curled herself up, the better to withdraw from the garden's constant, distracting small noises, and listen harder to what her father, striding forcefully back and forth behind the French windows just above her head, was saying about her to Caroline.

'Mope, mope, mope. That's all she ever seems to do nowadays.'

When Caroline responded with no more than a vague murmur of sympathy, Ione couldn't help guessing that she was, as usual, taking advantage of the fact that Professor Muffet was blind, to have a quick peep at the state of her hair in the mirror she kept propped against the file cards.

'Mope, mope, mope,' Professor Muffet said again. 'All day long.'

It was, Ione realized with relief, nothing new he was saying about her, nothing dreadful.

'Every school holiday is the same.'

Her father had begun to pace up and down the threadbare carpet, making the empty coffee mugs on his bookshelves rattle and jump for fright. 'She used to run around yelling, and fall out of trees, and swing on gates, and clutter the tables for days on end with enormous jigsaws of the Taj Mahal.'

He swivelled on the turn with an ease born of long practice, and began pacing the other half of the room, ending up dangerously close to the French windows.

'But now it's just seven whole weeks of mope, mope, mope!'

For all that she knew he couldn't see her, Ione shrank down further and cradled her knees closer. And it would never do to look too interesting, or Mandy might suddenly decide to heave herself up from where Caroline was using her for a footstool, and lumber over, giving her away.

Still peering in the mirror, Caroline slid one more grip into her hair, which was piled on her head in all manner of gravity-defying loops and whorls.

'She seems quite happy,' she said soothingly. 'She never complains.'

'That's not the *point*.' Professor Muffet raised his voice, enraged. 'Not the point *at all*. It's just not *good* for her. How can it be? It wouldn't be good for *anyone*.' The steady rattling from the mugs on the bookshelves caught his attention at last. On his next pace across, he swept them up and away to the blotter on his desk, where they stood clanking gently against one another instead. 'She never *does* anything. She never *goes* anywhere. And there's hardly another child over six years old around here for her to play with.'

'There's Ned,' said Caroline. She put her mirror down on top of the ginger biscuits and picked a nail file out of the marmalade jar in which she kept her blunted pencils.

'Ned must be twenty-four if he's a day,' Professor Muffet said, astonished.

'He acts like six,' said Caroline, surprisingly fondly, Ione thought, considering all the incredibly rude things she'd overheard her saying only the day before about her husband. But Caroline was famous for her mood swings. And, well aware how easily talk of Ned Hump turned into storms, Professor Muffet hastily steered the conversation back to the topic of his daughter.

'I only wish Ione would again.'

Outside on the steps, Ione allowed herself a tiny sigh. Would he ever be completely satisfied with her just the way she was? It hadn't happened yet. She didn't know about the very beginnings, when she was still tiny and her mother was alive; but as long as Ione could remember there had seemed to be no end to the things he could find in her to fret about. Maybe, since her mother died, he'd felt he really should be fretting for two . . .

Above her, Professor Muffet leaned his forehead for comfort against a cool pane of the window.

'I thought of taking her away to the sea,' he said. 'But we had that holiday last year, and anyway, I'm snowed under with work. We're *months* behind as it is.'

Turning, he waved a desperate arm towards the desk, which he knew, although he mercifully couldn't see it, was overflowing with essays his students had written that Caroline had not yet read aloud to him; interesting articles from the history journals; and letters that he was still waiting for her to transcribe into braille so he could read them himself again later – letters she had not yet even put at the bottom of her huge Things You Should Reply To At Once pile beside the notes she had twice tipped all over the floor and got out of order for the book he had been trying to write for two years.

Sometimes Professor Muffet wondered how someone of whom the agency spoke so highly, and was so good at braille, could get so far behind in her work. But then Ned had let it out that a lot of the problem stemmed from the fact that Caroline got distracted by the sight of her own pretty painted fingernails as they passed over the computer keyboard or the little raised braille dots.

But that couldn't explain *all* her errors. Or her forgetfulness. Or her untidiness. Or her stingy refusals to put the full amount of postage on anything. Or—

But she did have her skills, Professor Muffet reflected, pulling himself up. And soothing him when he was upset was supposed to be one of them. So he raised his head expectantly in her direction.

'She never complains,' Caroline now said again, soothingly. She started filing away calmly at her left thumbnail, which she had just noticed didn't quite match her right. 'If she's happy, what does it matter that she's not doing anything much with her time?'

Professor Muffet sat down heavily at his desk, and cradled his head in his hands. The ends of his prematurely greying hair fell inside one of the coffee mugs on the blotter and picked up some grounds. There was, Caroline noticed, a fresh dust smudge on his forehead that he must have picked up off the window panes. This wasn't the cleanest house in the village, she reflected, not for the first time. Professor Muffet never saw the grime; Ione never noticed it.

'Caroline,' Professor Muffet said as patiently as

he could over the faint rasping sounds she was making that were setting his teeth on edge. 'Caroline, think of it this way. I have a daughter – a healthy, intelligent daughter. A daughter who could be spending her time usefully taking chicken soup to the sick, or painting the fence, or learning Greek verbs—'

Outside on the steps, Ione shuddered. That was the one problem with eavesdropping: you heard such awful things.

'But what *is* she doing? Nothing. If you and Ned aren't around, she just wanders down to that old summerhouse and mopes. Well, there's more to living than just sitting around letting life slide past you, Caroline. Surely even *you* can see that.'

Caroline stopped filing her thumbnail and raised her head. She would have tossed it if he could have seen, and if all her careful loops and whorls wouldn't have fallen straight down. She hadn't cared for his 'Even *you* can see that' one bit. She thought she might mention the smudge on his forehead or the coffee grounds in his hair to pay him back; but she knew they wouldn't bother him. Half the time he didn't even shave, and his clothes were just awful to look at. And, anyhow, he had already risen and started his restless pacing again.

'Seven whole weeks. The holidays are seven weeks long.' The boards shuddered violently under Ione's legs, and she winced. 'Five of them have already gone, and what has she done so far? Written a letter to her Norwegian pen pal and made two trips to the dentist—'

He felt his watch.

'*If* she's remembered that that's where she's supposed to be by now, that is.'

'She would have helped Ned with his vegetable garden,' Caroline reminded him. 'If the reservoir hadn't got so low they stopped people watering their gardens. She planted all the turnips.'

'*Turnips!*' howled Professor Muffet in a tone of despair, flinging his arms wide and knocking the ginger biscuits flying towards Mandy, who gazed up in awe, as if they were manna descending. '*Turnips! Ned Hump!* Oh, *where* have I gone wrong? *Why* have I failed?'

Outside, Ione made a little face. Failed? Why failed? Surely it was a good idea for her and Ned to try to grow things. And if they chose to start with turnips, that was their business. In fact, Ione thought, if she chose to spend the whole of her holiday moping, that was her private business too, just as the old summerhouse was her own private place where she spent hours and hours inside or on the steps, quite happy and alone, thinking about things she'd overheard.

And there were plenty of those. After all, eavesdropping came naturally to someone whose father was in the habit of pacing up and down muttering to himself. She didn't even have to stay out of sight.

No, all she had to do was keep quiet, and it was hard to feel guilty for just doing that. And Professor Muffet hardly ever realized Ione was within hearing unless Mandy noticed her standing listening, perfectly still and silent, and bounded across in a rush of friendliness, unwittingly giving her away.

And for all the entreaties and warnings and scoldings that she had been subjected to on these occasions, Ione could not for the life of her see the harm in listening to other people talk. Sometimes she had learned things that saddened or scared her; but always, thinking it over again later, when the first shock of knowing had worn off, she thought she would rather have known than not known.

Sometimes she had overheard criticisms of her faults that hurt her feelings deeply; but more often than not she already suspected those same faults in herself and wondered if they showed. So it had usually come as a relief to find her father was already aware of them – that he could talk to himself about them from time to time in flurries of anxiety or exasperation, and then, immediately after, as if they mattered, but not all that much, bellow cheerfully to his daughter to come and keep him company on a walk to the village.

So, all in all, Ione was rather in favour of a good eavesdrop. That was, after all, how she came to learn that what Caroline wanted most in the world was a gold lamé umbrella. And how she knew Ned needed a gardening and cookery book. It was nice to get presents right – especially theirs. Ione adored Ned, and had become very fond indeed of Caroline. She'd learned so much from both of them. Caroline had taught her to put up her hair, in case she should ever want to do so. Ned had taught her a mnemonic for the colours of the spectrum – and then another, in case she should forget the first. And how to whistle. And hundreds of other things.

It had been, all in all, a lovely year. She had never been so happy. Summers before had seemed empty and endless – just 'seven whole weeks' of her father and herself and Mandy in the large ramshackle house that Professor Muffet had bought so cheaply because the bulge in the front wall that he never saw, and Doris thought perfect for trailing dog roses over, had looked so menacing to all the other prospective buyers.

But now a lot of the days were just like living in a real family. The photo of Ione's mother still sat, as it had as long as Ione could remember, on the piano. But now there was Caroline to push it aside to put the unfinished board games safely away till the next day; and now there was Ned to knock it over almost every afternoon with his elbow, and say 'Whoops, sorry,' to it when he came in with the tea tray. Ned and Caroline now rented a tiny flat in the vicarage grounds, above the old stables that overlooked the graveyard, and which could be creepy to run home from in the dark. But they only seemed to go there in the evenings. The rest of the time they were always in and out of Professor Muffet's house and garden. Caroline had the better excuse, but Ned could usually think of something. He was walking his new wife to work, or picking her up, or borrowing a history book from Professor Muffet, or asking Ione for a pencil sharpener or advice on his latest row with Caroline.

Professor Muffet never minded – he had been lonely, too, all these years – and Ione loved it.

So Ione sat on in the glaring sunlight that was baking the garden and baking her, and hugged her knees and waited for Caroline to sort things out, as Caroline always did. It always astonished Ione that Caroline could calm and console her father, but only get Ned into rages. Ione supposed it was something to do with the difference between friendship and love, but whenever she brought up the subject with Ned, he would groan and clutch his belly.

Ned hated love. It had, he told Ione, blighted his life, and he was heartily sick of it.

'It doesn't look easy,' Ione would agree, a little dubiously, swinging her legs against the tombstone she sat on, watching Ned chip away hopelessly with a bent trowel at the dried and ailing vegetable garden he had planted there with such high hopes in the damp early spring, out of sight of the vicar, behind the oldest graves which no one ever visited any more.

'*Easy?*' Ned would shout, straightening up to stare at her. '*Easy?* Easy has nothing whatever to do with it!'

Yes, that was the wonderful thing about Ned. Let drop a doubt or a thought, and he would almost always take it up. She'd spent a lot of time with him during this long hot summer that had crawled on and on without a single spell of rain. He, at least, seemed to accept her the way she was. And so, largely because of him, she had enjoyed every single day of these five whole weeks about which her father sounded so despairing. How could two people who were each other's closest relations have such differing views of the same thing? For inside the room, Professor Muffet was still muttering, 'Ned Hump – ha! *Turnips!*' to himself over and over above the faint rasp of Caroline's nail file.

But clearly the flurry was over. There was no point in delaying any longer.

Shaking her head so her hair fell away from her face for the first time since she settled on the steps, Ione Muffet hooked up her sandal straps with one finger, and slipped silently down across the caked and yellowing lawn towards the wicket gate.

It was always possible that someone else had forgotten an appointment, after all, and Mr Hooper was now only half an hour behind schedule.

Chapter 12

Ione walked through the village by her father's side, still in a daze from the anaesthetic Mr Hooper had given her. She had felt quite ready to set off for home just a few minutes before, when she was sitting resting afterwards, in his hallway. But now her knees had begun to shake, and her eyes kept filling with a strange fuzziness. By the time they reached the short cut through the graveyard, where Ned and Caroline were standing under a yew, kissing hello long and loudly after a whole day's separation, Ione's legs were trembling so fiercely that her father made his daughter stop for a moment, and let Mandy off the leading rein.

Ned stopped pulling the pins out of Caroline's hair and turned to peer in Ione's face.

'You look *awful*,' he said to her. 'Lie down.

Have a little rest on this nice, dry, comfy grave. Breathe very deeply.'

Ione lay flat on her back, starfish-fashion, on the tomb he had offered her: that of Martha Cuddlethwaite, born August 5th 1721, died December 17th 1801. She closed her eyelids against the harsh, dancing patterns of sunlight that broke through the leaves just above her, onto her face, making her eyes hurt almost as much as her mouth did. The mushy hole in her gum, where the tooth had been only half an hour before, had begun to throb. The pain was clearly seeping through without much trouble now.

She dabbed at the new, sore gap tentatively with her tongue, which felt huge and clumsy, like a predatory slug creeping around in a vast wet cavern. Her brain teemed with violent, swirling colours. The tombstone chilled her spine through her thin cotton shirt; but the rest of her, especially her head, was getting hotter and hotter. She gave the quietest little gasp as her tongue prodded a shade too deeply into her gum, and wondered, for an awful moment, if she were going to disgrace herself and be sick all over the grass.

On the next grave – Thomas Morton, born June 2nd 1790, died September 22nd 1851 – her father lay with his eyes, too, tightly closed. The sunlight didn't bother Professor Muffet at all. But he had heard her tiny noise and screwed his own eyes up more as a grimace of sympathy than for protection. It was the first time he had ever accompanied anyone who was having a tooth out, and he had found the sheer nastiness of the business quite harrowing. Secretly, he had hoped he would miss it. After all, Ione had said her appointment was for three o'clock, and it was not until nearly four that he and Mandy had arrived to walk her home. First, there had been all that clinking and chinking and gathering together of pointed instruments. Then he had caught himself imagining how Ione must be sitting, in that huge monstrous chair, with her head forced back and her mouth forced open.

There were times when Professor Muffet was glad he missed out on seeing things. More often, he thought that the pictures which swam uninvited into his head were probably far worse than the real thing. He remembered the soft clunk the tooth made when it was dropped in a tin bowl, and pulled Mandy closer for comfort.

She dug her chin deeper into his stomach, and began to wheeze.

'You should have that dog seen to,' said Ned. 'She sounds awful. I think she needs oiling.'

He was leaning back against a pillar – *In Remembrance of Captain Flook, 1702–1732* – with his arm around Caroline, who had begun plaiting their hair together, tidily and carefully, two strands of her yellow to one of Ned's dark, because hers was longer. He suspected that she was doing it too tightly, and that she had started way too far up. Last time she had done it, it had taken Ione an hour to unpick them. But today she didn't look up to the job. He supposed he and Caroline would stay plaited for ever since his wife was too vain to cut tufts in her hair to release him.

But it was a hot and breathless day, and he didn't have the energy to stop her. So he just moved his head a little, hoping to loosen himself.

'Keep still,' Caroline told him. 'You're making my head hurt.'

'My tooth hurts more,' complained Ione suddenly from on top of her tomb.

'Your hole, you mean,' said Ned. 'Your hole hurts. But holes in you are, by definition, not a part of you, and therefore they can't hurt. So you're perfectly all right really.'

While Ione was finding the flaw in this, Caroline asked: 'Why did Mr Hooper take it out, anyway?' Wetting her fingers, she twisted the last inch of Ned's hair into a fine point, and knotted it neatly out of sight with her own two ends. 'There!'

'He said he had to take it out to make room,' said Ione. 'He said my jaw was too small for all my teeth because I ate nothing but feet.'

'Did he really?' asked Ned, astonished. 'What an extraordinary thing for a reputable dentist to say.'

'He said everyone ate far too many feet nowadays.'

'I don't,' said Ned. 'I don't eat any feet. No one in our family does. Did you eat feet, before we met?' he asked Caroline politely.

'No,' said Caroline thoughtfully. 'I can't say that I did.'

'There you are,' said Ned triumphantly. 'Here, on an on-the-spot poll of two people, you have unanimous agreement that feet are not part of the average household's weekly diet. You are unusual, Ione, in eating feet. Perhaps you're being cheated by your butcher. Perhaps your butcher is a mass murderer, who sends bits of his victims to your

163

house, banking on the fact that your father won't be able to see these strange cuts of meat for what they are, namely, feet.'

He broke off a piece of dried-up grass and began to chew it. 'I'm surprised at *you*, though, Ione. A girl of your intelligence should be able to recognize a stewed foot when it's put in front of you, however cunningly done over in wine sauce and sprinkled with chopped-up chives it may be. I'm disappointed in you.'

'I don't eat feet,' said Ione.

'I beg your pardon. I thought you said you did.'

'I didn't say I did. Mr Hooper said I did.'

'Well, why did Mr Hooper say you did, then?'

'Mr Hooper didn't say she did,' said Professor Muffet, raising himself up on an elbow just long enough to set things straight. 'He didn't say she ate feet at all. He didn't say anybody ate feet. What he said was that all the foods everybody eats nowadays are effete.'

'Oh,' said Ione.

'Ah, yes,' said Ned. 'Well, that's quite different.'

Ione sat up on her tombstone and swung herself round till her legs dangled down over the side. She still felt strange. Colours and patterns still rolled and swirled inside her head, and she felt light all over; but the pain in her mouth had now settled down to a steady, manageable throb.

She tried to explain.

'He said that if people hadn't stopped gnawing at raw turnips, their jaws wouldn't have become trophies and—'

'Atrophied,' corrected Professor Muffet.

'And got smaller,' continued Ione, ignoring him beautifully. 'And then we could have fitted in all the teeth we grow without their getting all squashed up and crooked. He says the problem is bound to get worse not better unless we all go back to chewing raw turnips.'

'I thought you were still too woozy to hear a thing through all that,' said her father, amazed. It never failed to astonish him how much Ione always seemed to pick up of other people's conversations.

'I think I'd rather have all my teeth pulled out,' said Caroline, and then, when Ned laughed, she shrieked. 'Ouch!'

Ione stared at her.

'Look what you've *done*,' she said to Caroline, in horror. 'You've done it *again*. It's worse than last time. You've done it right the way down from the top. You're completely knotted together.'

'One flesh,' said Ned mildly, smiling.

'Two fools,' rejoined Ione.

'Have they plaited themselves up again?' asked Professor Muffet, surprised. 'I'd have thought they'd have known better after last time.'

'I shan't even *try* not to hurt when I undo you,' said Ione, still cross.

'Don't bother,' advised Ione's father. 'Leave them. Let them stay here. They can crawl together in excruciating pain to Ned's dried-up vegetable garden every now and again, and root up a couple of turnips to gnaw at in their death agony.'

'The turnips never came up,' said Ned gloomily.

'Turnips don't,' said Caroline. 'Turnips stay down.'

'Nothing came up,' said Ned. 'It's not surprising. The ground was baked so hard when Ione and I planted the last time that we could hardly get the seeds in.'

'They ruined my grandmother's knitting needles trying,' put in Caroline. 'All her eights, she says, and a couple of long sixes.' She gazed as far round at her husband as she could, and fondly squeezed his fingers.

'It didn't do any good,' said Ned. 'You'd need a

jumbo-sized tractor to make a dent in that vegetable garden. The soil is like cement. I kept hoping it would rain.'

'Didn't we all?' said Professor Muffet wistfully, thinking of his ruined lawn.

'They never even *tried* to grow,' said Ned, freshly outraged at the memory. 'They never even tried to *start*, let alone to grow up out of the ground. If there's no water, then they just won't *try*.'

Ione looked across the graveyard to the unshaded cleared patch by the wall which they were talking about. It had been so fresh and green and rich and brown when they had started it. But that hadn't lasted long. And now it was about as unpromising a vegetable garden as you could hope to see. There was nothing there. It was just a strip of yellowing, flat, baked earth. Two deep cracks ran zigzag across the right-hand corner, and a broken trowel leaned against the wall. There were a couple of bent and rusting knitting needles lying about, but nothing alive.

It could be a vegetable garden from one of those countries where the monsoon sometimes fails, she thought. She didn't know exactly what their vegetable gardens would look like; but she

ANNE FINE

was sure that, like Ned's, they would look dry as
a bone, unshaded and dusty.

She looked over at Ned, leaning cool and idle
in the shade of Captain Flook's pillar, with his
head on Caroline's shoulder, stroking her soft,
bare arm gently. He wasn't as thin as he was when
she first met him, and she supposed, proudly, that
since she had given him that gardening and
cookery book, he had been eating better. He used
to wolf down entire chocolate fudge cakes in one
sitting without even noticing, and still have room
for a huge meal straight after, if anyone should
happen to offer him one. They had all been quite
amazed at the amounts he could eat.

She wondered what he would have been like if
he'd grown up somewhere poorer in the world
instead, depending on a vegetable garden like that
for his meals. He'd be thinner, and much darker,
and his eyes would almost certainly be brown, not
green. Otherwise, he'd look much the same,
though. She could picture him easily.

She closed her eyes for a moment. The swirling
patterns in her befuddled brain coalesced
suddenly, and she could actually see him there,
out in the sickening sunlight. He was wearing a
stripy, tattered shirt. He often wore stripy tattered

shirts anyhow, here in the village; but this one, she just knew, was ripped and shredded in a different, a more distressing, way.

He had propped a long heavy hoe over his bony shoulders, and he was standing on the edge of a vast plain that ran away and away and off into a massive overhanging sky that it was hurting his eyes to look at. He wiped his damp forehead with a filthy hand, leaving streaks of greenish caked-dry earth across his anxious face, and then he shaded his eyes and hunched his shoulders the tiniest bit forward. He was peering to try and see clouds in that glaring, glassy sky, Ione realized, and it was very important to him.

Then he turned towards her and looked straight into her eyes without speaking. He looked drained and shaken. Ever so slightly, he shrugged his shoulders.

'What will you *do*, then?' Ione cried out aloud, forgetting in her pain-soaked confusion that the pictures in her head were hers alone, that no one else had seen them.

The real Ned narrowed his eyes at her curiously. She looked quite ashen, he thought.

'What do you *think* we'll do?' he said. 'We can't *starve* to death, can we? We'll catch the bus to

Sainsbury's like everyone else does, and pay a king's ransom for someone else's dried-up turnip to gnaw on.'

Ione's eyes widened. She stared at him blankly. Sainsbury's? Where *he* lived? *Surely* not. Surely he *would* just starve.

Tears pricked behind her eyes, and she swallowed.

Just then, her head cleared once and for all. She understood exactly what had happened. In her strange mood, she had confused the two Neds. The one who had answered her was the real one, cheerful, well-fed and unconcerned. But it was to the other, darker Ned that she had really voiced the question. And she wondered for an awful moment just how *he* would have replied.

'I think,' said Ione, slipping off the high gravestone onto the dried and crackling grasses that scratched at her ankles, 'I think I should like to go home now.'

Chapter 13

It was several days before Ione saw Ned again. The afternoon in the graveyard had set her thinking, and she had been busy doing something special of her own. But on Friday morning, hearing his tuneless, lugubrious rendering of *Non Nobis Domine* float in through the lattices, she rose from where she was sitting on the summerhouse floor, amid a sea of papers that she had gathered around her, and watched him curiously through the creepers that had become so thin and grey and brittle in the last dry weeks that they no longer hid the summerhouse from view.

He strolled through the gate and across the lawn towards the house. With each long lanky stride, he swung a little bright red case up and down. It was the case in which he carried around the examination papers he was supposed to be

ANNE FINE

marking for money, for his summer job; but
usually he couldn't even decipher them without
somebody else's help. As he neared the study
windows, he switched from *Non Nobis Domine*
to *Animal Crackers in My Soup*, whistled at top
speed and extremely cheerfully. Ione was
surprised. She hadn't thought he would be up to
whistling yet awhile, unless he and Caroline had
somehow ended their furious drawn-out quarrel
over the plaited hair. And from what she had
overheard Caroline telling her father the day
before, during one of their frequent tea-breaks,
there seemed very little chance of that.

So Ione supposed that Ned was just putting a
brave face on things, acting so cheery and forthright as he passed by the house, just in order to
discomfit Caroline, who was probably watching
him covertly right this moment over her braille-
type keyboard.

Ione sighed. Sometimes she wished Ned
wouldn't overdo everything quite so badly. She
could just tell, from the way he was swinging the
little red case, that everything inside it would
have broken away from its paperclip moorings,
and shuffled itself up horribly. Usually Ione was
delighted to leave off whatever she was doing to

help Ned sort his papers out again, ink colour by ink colour, handwriting by handwriting, page by unnumbered page; but today she was busy sorting papers of her own.

So she stepped back further into the shadows of the summerhouse, where the slim bars of sunlight couldn't light her through the lattices, and she hoped for almost the first time ever that today he'd go straight to the house.

Crossing the Muffets' shrivelled lawn, Ned peered curiously through a strange little round cleared patch on one of the dust-filmed panes of the French windows, and saw Caroline sitting as usual curled up in an armchair, reading aloud, with a half-peeled, but unchewed banana in one hand, and a sheaf of papers in the other. Professor Muffet was lying on his stomach on the rug, scratching Mandy's ears, and listening.

Ned pushed the French windows open, inwards.

'... Thereby leading to the more acceptable trade agreements of 1626, 1627 and 1629 between the two sovereignties, marred only by the so-called Carrot War of 1628 ...' Caroline read on steadily, ignoring her husband's presence, although Ned knew she must have heard the door creak.

Then, changing her mind, she looked up in order to stare right through him as though he wasn't there. 'And the General Vegetable Embargo of 1630,' she added, in a tone of voice so wintry that it sent shivers down Professor Muffet's spine.

Ned sighed. They had been having a very difficult time.

After Ione had left the graveyard so abruptly, leaving them as hopelessly entwined as they later proved to be, there had passed what Ned still thought of as the very worst hour he had ever yet spent in Caroline's company. And given her natural quick temper, which, he sometimes suspected, she made few attempts to curb, this had made it an extremely nasty hour indeed.

First, she had blamed Ned for the fact that they were in the predicament in the first place. He'd come to his own defence hotly, pointing out that it was she, and not he, who had knotted them together. Indeed, he had had no idea what she was about until it was too late, and she was half-way down to his neck. He had assumed, in his innocence, that she was merely stroking his hair, that these were fond, tender caresses that he could feel above his left ear.

Caroline came back at him with a stunning complaint. If his hair had been longer, she said, she could have tied a neat bow at the end of the plait that would have been easy to undo, instead of the screwed-up little knot she had been reduced to. It was unarguably his fault.

At this, Ned had gasped.

Caroline became more and more unreasonable and foul tempered. And as she became angrier, she shook her head more and more fiercely, till the discomfort Ned was feeling turned into pain, and his brave winces into bitter howls of protest.

At this point, Caroline ordered Professor Muffet along to Waley's for olive oil to rub on the plait, insisting that this would make the hair simplicity itself to unravel. Professor Muffet had come back with soya bean oil. All the shoppers in Waley's grocery, backed up by Mrs Waley herself, had insisted that, at less than half the price, it was by far the better buy.

They tried it. Professor Muffet worked it into the plait, rubbing gently with his fingers. He told Ione afterwards how remarkable it was that, after the first couple of 'ouches' from each of them while he got his bearings, he could tell exactly whose strands of hair he was handling merely from the texture. Once the oil was well worked in, though, it all felt the same, and rather nasty.

Caroline spent the next few minutes coming unwillingly to the conclusion that the plan had failed. She wasted a few more moments berating Professor Muffet for the fact that her hair now smelled of soya beans.

Professor Muffet stood by, helpless, holding the leaking bottle of oil and wondering what to do next.

In the end, Ned had asserted himself more than usual. He told Caroline shortly to hand over her bag. There were bound to be nail scissors, he said, in the bag of someone who spent so much of her life caring for her nails.

Caroline refused point blank, kicking the little green tapestry purse as far out of his reach as she was able, into the undergrowth around the Merchant-Truckles' stone angel. Cutting off the end of the plait would, she insisted furiously, make her all tufty.

Ned braced himself against the excruciating pain that he knew was coming. If he didn't do something, he now realized, they would be plaited together all night. So with immense courage and fortitude he forced his way over to the bag, step by fighting, screaming step, dragging his truculent wife along with him.

The pain was almost unbearable. Tears flooded his eyes and he whimpered softly. Professor Muffet, who could not stand to hear these goings-on, at last thought to order Mandy to fetch the bag which he himself could not see. But at the first whimper from Ned, Mandy had slunk off, terrified, and was now hiding behind the vicar's broken lawn mower, pretending not to hear and refusing to come out.

Ned persisted. Caroline hung back, in spite of the agony, with all her strength.

Ned lost his temper just thinking about how vain she was.

'If you don't give up struggling,' he hissed at her fiercely between his teeth, 'I am going to stab you to death with those nail scissors when I finally get hold of them. Captain Flook's pillar will *drip* with your blood. The Merchant-Truckles' angel will get splattered all over. And my last act of revenge on you will be to cut the hair on your mangled corpse all scraggy before the police come and get me.'

Caroline faltered, then gave in. She burst into noisy tears.

Professor Muffet had done the neatest job he could with the nail scissors, cutting as far down the plait as possible, and unravelling what was left of each of them carefully.

Caroline continued to weep throughout. Ned, freed, stood and shook himself gratefully. He looked down at his wife, crumpled up against Captain Flook's pillar, crying miserably over a few strands of matted, oily plait.

'You are *obsessed* with your appearance,' he told her sternly. 'It's *disgusting*.'

She stopped crying at that. She started yelling instead.

'*You* were obsessed with my appearance once, too,' she shouted. 'You didn't find yourself so disgusting.'

'Regard for Beauty is a Virtue,' Ned said proudly. 'Whereas Vanity is a Sin.'

Professor Muffet was shocked at Ned's temerity.

Caroline slapped Ned's face.

Neither had spoken to the other since. They had each gone to enormous pains to be spiteful. Ned had taken all the housekeeping money from the cracked china pig on the sideboard, and cooked himself delicious aromatic meals from the cookery book Ione had given them for Christmas. He took great pleasure in eating them, wordlessly, before Caroline each evening, just as she returned tired and hungry from working at the Muffets'.

Pretending she didn't care in the slightest, Caroline had lived on cheese sandwiches. But she had had her revenge. She'd left the fat hairy spider that had come up the drain in search of water sitting in the kitchen sink, untroubled. Ned, who had been mortally afraid of spiders since childhood, had had to use the bathroom to wash all the dishes and saucepans and mixing bowls dirtied during the creation of his lavish meals, carrying them back and forth interminably. If he slackened, and left one unwashed on the draining board, Caroline would heave it out of the window onto the cobbles beneath within minutes of coming back into the flat. By Thursday, Ned was prudently confining himself to rich-odoured casseroles simmered in one pot.

It had been a dismal and discouraging time for both of them. And it was, Ned thought, unfortunate that he now had to start peace negotiations with his wife by asking her a favour.

'I need your help, Caroline,' he now said, tapping at the side of the little red case with his fingers. He heard a sudden suspicious rustling inside, and hoped all the papers were still sitting neatly in the alphabetical name order in which the examination board had thoughtfully arranged them. 'These have to be marked by tomorrow, and I can read hardly any of the writing.' He had been trying all week, he reflected, when he hadn't been cooking.

Ever so slightly, Caroline raised one eyebrow at him. Then, with a sudden vicious chomp of her sharp white teeth, she took a very large bite of banana and chewed it, slowly, slowly, till it was gone.

'Tough,' she told him sweetly.

Ned shuddered, turned and left.

He'd known she wouldn't respond at once. She had far too much pride for that. So had he. If the examination board hadn't been sending him nasty little messages all week, he would never have come to the Muffets' to ask for her help in the first place.

And it had been a clever move, making the request in front of her employer. Ned reckoned that had saved him from a goodly spate of wrath.

How long had they been married now? Long enough for him to know that her refusal to help out would make her feel mean. If he followed it up by cooking her favourite mackerel supper tonight, she would have to make the next move.

A couple more skirmishes, he thought to himself, a little more happily. Two more days at the very most.

He went off towards the summerhouse to find Ione. She could read bad writing too. She had been reading aloud to her father the letters sent to him by learned people for years.

Chapter 14

When he pushed open the warped little door and walked in on her, Ione took the pencil from between her teeth and unpuckered her brow to smile up at him. She was, after all, pleased to see him, she realized. She needed his advice.

Ione had been working all the morning, doing a vast number of tedious arithmetical calculations and a lot of hard thinking; but now she had reached an impasse. Banking on all Ned's extra knowledge and experience, she asked him: 'Which would you rather be given, Ned? A pregnant goat or eight hundred and thirty-two chicks.'

'Eight hundred and thirty-two chicks,' said Ned without a moment's hesitation, shifting some of the papers aside with his foot and dropping down beside her on the cool flagstones. 'I would take the chicks. Eight hundred and thirty-two sounds like a fair few to handle; but I already have a goat, even though, as far as I know, she isn't pregnant. Indeed, I made the serious mistake of marrying her.'

Ione giggled.

'Are you two still at it?' she asked. 'Dad will be pleased. He's hoping to clear his work backlog if you keep it up all through next week.'

'I beg your pardon,' Ned said icily.

Ione, all unheeding, went on to explain.

'Dad says if it hadn't been for all the rows you two have had since you got married, his desk would probably have collapsed by now. He says your ill-matched temperaments are the saving of his career. He says he feels very sorry for you both, being so miserable and all that whenever it happens, but it's an ill wind that blows nobody any good. He says Caroline becomes a whirlwind of activity whenever you quarrel. He said she cleared an entire month's correspondence off the windowsill in two days when you had that big fight over which of the goldfish to keep. He says he always knows the minute you two have made it up again, because she just goes back to mooning and sitting and painting her toenails all day.'

'Well,' said Ned. 'Well, well, well. He says all that, does he?'

'Yes,' said Ione simply. 'Quite often.'

Ned's curiosity battled with his marital pride for a few moments, and won with ease.

'How does he know she paints her toenails?' he asked, intrigued. 'She doesn't *know* he knows. She thinks she's very clever the way she slips in all that nail varnishing and hair curling and eyebrow shaping in front of his very eyes.'

'He may be blind, but he's not daft,' said Ione. 'And he can smell the varnish. At first, he thought it was pear drops, and asked if he could have one, and was very hurt when she denied having any. But then a few days afterwards he found out, when she kicked Mandy in a frightful rage.'

'She's *always* done that,' said Ned Hump. 'She's notorious at the agency for being a secret guide dog kicker. Your father is the very first person who hasn't sacked her for it.'

'He thought it was over-enthusiasm for her work,' Ione said. 'She had such good references. He didn't realize everyone was just trying to fob her off on him because he's not choosy. He thought Caroline kept kicking Mandy because she will keep trampling all over the papers and books on the floor. But then he realized that Caroline didn't care at all about that. She tramples all over them too, he says. In shoes. But one day Caroline really gave herself away. She really lost her temper. Usually she just kicks Mandy sneakily under the table. But this time she kicked her half way out of the French windows, shouting, "Smelly rotten dog hairs all over my toenails. Now I shall have to start all over again!"'

A smile of pride and delight crept over Ned Hump's features. But catching Ione's stern, inquisitive look, he banished it at once.

'Your father has exemplary tolerance, allowing my wife to idle her days away in his study, preening herself,' he said. 'When you remember he even pays her for doing it, his behaviour can only be regarded as saintly.'

Relieved, Ione relaxed.

'She really is a goat,' added Ned.

He got to his feet and started prowling around the small space like a caged beast, peering through the latticework. All this talk about the person he was quarrelling with was unsettling him. He picked up one of Ione's pencils and began teasing a spider in the web over the door. It was the tiniest spider he had ever seen, and he took his revenge on it for the big fat hairy one that was still in his kitchen sink. Pressing the pencil point down just firmly enough on an important web strand to bounce but not break it, he burst out balefully at Ione: 'What a goat she is! I'm surprised you're thinking of getting me another. I'm only allowed to be married to one goat at once.'

'This one isn't for you,' said Ione. 'It's for someone else.'

It was for Ned really, she thought, in a way.

Ione had, in the last few days, taken even herself by surprise. She had decided to do something with the last two weeks left to her of her summer holiday – something to help the other Ned she had seen suddenly that day in the graveyard: the other, darker Ned on whose land the rains would not fall, and whose vegetable garden lay rutted and hard, like bits of broken china. She didn't know quite where the idea of actually helping him had sprung from, and she hadn't wasted much time wondering about that. For once it had come to her that she should – and that seemed so simple and obvious now that she had no doubts about it at all. The main problem had been to work out exactly how. After all, she hadn't much time. Five whole weeks of her holiday had already gone by. There was no time to lose.

So the very next day she had gone into Eveling on the bus by herself, without a word to anyone. She had asked and found the way to the Oxfam shop she had heard the villagers talk about, across from the fish market, on the Balls Ferry Road. She had spent hours there; and behind the fancy blouses and the sturdy winter coats, the carton of baby bonnets, the trays of kitchen equipment that overflowed down onto the jewellery shelf, the pillowcases and sheets folded neatly in the wooden cradle, the shelves of books and comics, and the sky-blue tricycle on which someone had balanced a box of assorted plant seeds – behind all this, Ione had found a rack of free pamphlets, all about countries she had never even heard of and interesting facts she could never have guessed.

A quarter of the people in the world used up nearly four-fifths of everything that came from it – food, oil, minerals – everything. That wasn't fair. Ione read about a young cotton farmer in Africa called Kabula. Kabula could grow enough cotton to make hundreds of the local dresses. There was a photo of her wearing one, and it looked bright and comfortable. But when Kabula came to sell her harvest every year, the money she earned was only enough to buy one dress for herself.

Grow enough for hundreds? Earn enough for *one*?

It seemed so very unfair. Ione could scarcely believe it. Perhaps there had been some mistake in the printing. Looking round for someone to ask, she caught sight of a poster.

ONE IN FOUR CHILDREN
GO TO BED HUNGRY
EACH NIGHT

One *in four*? Every *night*? Ione stared at it, appalled. That couldn't be a mistake. People would notice an error in a poster. The longer she stared, the worse Ione felt. She couldn't have gone to bed hungry more than three or four times in her whole life. And that had always been her own choice – from temper, or sulking, or feeling a bit queasy.

No. It was clearly time for a good think.

Ione sat down on the edge of a trunk of garden tools and reached for one pamphlet after another.

She was still buried deep in them when the lady called over to her that they were closing and she had to leave.

The lady was helpful. She gave Ione a bag to put all the papers and pamphlets in to take home. And during the bus-ride home, Ione drew out her pieces of paper again, one by one, still engrossed.

One, in particular, caught her attention. It had a photograph of a fisherman standing delightedly by the side of a rough-looking canoe he had obviously just pulled out of a wide and glistening lake. He held a large silver-bellied fish up in triumph in one hand, and a strangely shaped net in the other. His children were all around him, happily leaping and hopping about, wet, brown and shiny. The slogan underneath the photograph read:

Give a man a fish and you feed him for a day;
Teach a man to fish and you feed him for a lifetime.

Ione found this photograph comforting. The problems, she had realized, were overwhelming. But looking at the fisherman, she could see it was not hopeless.

Ione pushed the pamphlet back in the bag and sat without moving for the rest of the journey. She gazed, unseeing, at the fields and hedges and tractors that flashed by.

She was thinking hard.

These were the papers that were now scattered all around her and Ned. They contained the facts that all her arithmetic of the morning had been about.

There were about five hundred people living in the village, she guessed. If each one of them gave her only the same amount her father handed over each week for her pocket money, then she would have enough to buy any one of a number of interesting things that would help someone like the other, darker Ned. She had been finding it really hard to choose, in fact, when Ned Hump walked in on her.

'Suppose we raised five hundred times my allowance,' she told him. 'That's seven weighing scales for baby clinics, or a pregnant goat to give milk, or one thousand two hundred and eighty polio vaccinations, or eight hundred and fifty-three baby chicks, or thirteen crop sprayers, or half a candle-making unit, or one sixth of a water tank, or a lot of corrugated iron roofing, or two-and-a-bit bullocks.'

Ned stared at her, astonished. Her eyes were shining, she was flushed with excitement. She was a changed person, he thought.

'Which bit?' he asked.

Ione threw down her list and jumped to her feet. 'I'm choosing today,' she told him firmly. 'I'm not stewing over it all any longer. There's not enough time. So what do you think? What do you choose?'

'I choose bullocks,' said Ned. 'You choose bits.'

Ione smiled happily. 'There,' she said to herself softly. 'That's that.'

Ned took a deep breath. 'In return for all my help so far,' he wheedled, 'and all the help I shall give in the future, will you do me the favour of deciphering all the writing in this suitcase?'

He kicked it. Again, he heard that suspicious rustling from inside, but again he ignored it.

'I shall leave the case with you, Ione,' he said. 'You have until dawn tomorrow to decode all those essays.'

'Like the Miller's daughter,' said Ione.

'Exactly!' cried Ned. 'Caroline will serve admirably as Rumpelstiltskin without a trace of acting effort on her part; and I, the king's son, will be back in the morning.'

Kneeling, he attacked the catches, and flung open the suitcase. But it was upside down, and his piles of loose papers flew out and up all over, like freed birds, as a number of small silver paperclips clattered onto the flagstones.

The sheets of paper, scrawled all over with assorted handwritings, sailed around the summer-house, dipping and fluttering as they caught the breeze that blew in through the lattice-work, weaving and threading. On their leisurely return to the ground, they mixed themselves up thoroughly with Ione's pamphlets, and dirtied themselves on the floor.

Ned and Ione watched, open-mouthed, in silence. Then Ned groaned.

'Oh, no,' he said, and put his head in his hands. 'Oh no. Oh, no. Oh, no.'

As they knelt, side by side, sorting out the different inks from the different nib-widths, the fat letters from the loopy, pamphlets from exam papers, Ned snatched at a sheet of paper from Ione's pile.

'This pamphlet's *scented*,' he told her, astonished. 'Here, smell. It's Chest-rub, by Vick.'

He sniffed appreciatively. 'I wear it often myself.' Peering at the paper more closely, he asked her: 'What is this, anyway, Ione? "One Hundred and One Ways of Making Money for Oxfam"? How extraordinary. I didn't know there were one hundred and one ways of making money for anything.'

As he read down the list, his face became more and more anxious. 'I hope you're not thinking of trying any of these,' he said sternly to Ione.

'I thought one or two of them sounded quite fun,' she answered wistfully.

'No, no, no,' said Ned firmly, tearing the list into tiny shreds before her eyes, just to be sure. 'You stick with a Bring and Buy sale. They're safe. Everyone knows what they are. If you once start on any of these new-fangled things, like Sponsored Walks and Sponsored Fasts, you'll get in big trouble. One small slip in the planning and you'll have some idiot toddler walking up the fast lane of the by-pass because no one told him to stop, or some old lady fasting herself to death to spite all the neighbours who sponsored her. Oh, no. No, no, no. You be careful. You don't want to end up in court. You stick with a Bring and Buy sale and you'll be perfectly safe.'

ANNE FINE

Ione gathered up the last of her pamphlets.
'A Bring and Buy sale it is, then,' she said.
She knew better than to argue with Ned in this mood.

Chapter 15

I one sat back on her heels and admired her handiwork. Spread over the kitchen floor were eight large posters. Each of the posters was different. But all bore, somewhere or other, this information.

HUGE BRING AND BUY SALE

Toys, clothes, things, nice food and helium balloons

Saturday, 4th September

At 2.30 pm promptly,

In the Church Hall.

Every item cheap at double the price.
Very Worthy Cause.

Some were written in big bold letters, others in flowery script. One was all red, another navy-blue. One had a geometric border of rhomboids and triangles; one had rows of bright daisies all along the top and bottom.

It was Ned Hump, in his purely advisory capacity, who had suggested that she put in the helium balloons.

'Helium balloons are an idea of genius,' he told her. 'Every child in the village will be there. I can picture it now.' He sat down on the rather grubby kitchen floor beside her, and leaned back against the oven door. His face went all dreamy.

'Outside the church hall there'll be a long, winding queue of shrieking, impatient toddlers, and harassed, exhausted mums. The queue will *creep* forward, because each child in turn who gets to the front will take an *age* to make up its mind what colour balloon it wants. Half of them will drop their money into the gutter. The pavement will be *a-glitter* with lost pennies. The sky will be *crazy* with accidentally let-go balloons. Children will stand there, tears streaming down their anxious little faces, torn in an agony of in-decision. Shall I keep screaming while I watch that beautiful red balloon that I stood in a queue for twenty minutes to get, float right up out of my sight? Or shall I start whining and pestering my mother right now for the money to buy another?'

He shifted his back slightly against the warm oven door to get more comfortable, while Ione listened, entranced, putting the tops back on her felt pens.

'And here and there all afternoon inside the church hall itself, people will scream and start as one balloon after another pops with an enormous *bang*: this one poked by a carelessly wielded umbrella, for it's bound to be pouring with rain outside; that one allowed to rise just a fraction too high, and caught by a splinter in the rafters.' He wriggled in ecstasy. 'Oh, I can see it now. And by tea-time, all the very little ones, who can't quite talk yet, and couldn't *explain* that they were snivelling all afternoon because the string was tied far too tightly around their chubby wrists, will have got gangrene and have to have their hands cut off.'

He smiled ecstatically. 'Oh, yes. Helium balloons are an idea of genius.'

Ione smiled at him in rapt admiration.

'You're a monster,' she said fondly.

She gathered her posters into a pile. Ned

reached for the top one and looked at it more closely.

Tucked in each corner was a drawing of a dripping, gummy, recently extracted tooth. Each of the teeth was done in blackish pencil and nicely shaded, but the blood was done in violent red felt pen.

Ned eyed Ione curiously.

'What nice decorations,' he said to her casually. 'Beautifully drawn. Eye-catching, even. Quite a talking point, in fact. But why teeth?'

'It's for Mr Hooper to display in his waiting room,' said Ione proudly. 'It's special. They're all special. They're all made particularly for where they're to be displayed. I've spent a lot of time on them.'

'Yes,' said Ned, pulling the pile of posters towards him, and leafing through them, one by one. 'Yes, I can see that you have.'

After the dentist's was the one for the bus shelter. This one had a little frieze along the bottom. The right-hand side showed several irate villagers standing tapping their watches, and pointing angrily to the bus timetable pinned on the bus shelter wall. The left-hand side showed the bus driver sitting comfortably against the terminus wall, finishing a crossword while the bus sat idly behind him.

The poster Ione had designed for the Muffets' own gate was plainer. It just showed Professor Muffet standing proudly behind a table full of what appeared to be useless, broken junk, selling off his guide dog for a handful of coins to two small children.

It was a good likeness of her father, Ned thought to himself, and smiled.

Half of the poster for the primary school was devoted to a picture of the headmistress, Mrs Tallentire, being swept up and away from the playground by a huge bunch of helium balloons, while the infants and juniors waved and cheered.

The post office's poster showed a red pillar box with letters overflowing from its mouth, standing knee-deep in a sea of unfranked letters and packets. On its square white plate which gave the daily collection times, Ione had printed in tiny, but quite readable letters: *Collections: 4th December, 4 pm; 27th April, 12 noon.*

'That one's going to go down very well,' observed Ned.

The poster to be displayed on the churchyard gate was printed in spiky gothic lettering. Ione had used only dark cypress green and grey. In the centre, she'd drawn the silhouette of a crooked, tumbledown church, and inside this frame she'd drawn the vicar, easily recognizable from his height and his bad stoop, slinking away from the Bring and Buy sale with a pile of toys, clothes and nice food gathered up in his cassock. A helium balloon floated above him, fastened by a string to one of his fingers.

Ned shook his head in wonder.

The pub's poster showed a crowd of smiling drunkards, all ages and sizes, mostly leaning over the tables, fast asleep. One or two, who were still awake, were brandishing their empty tankards hopefully in the direction of the beer pumps. But behind the bar, the landlord stood calmly wiping glasses with a checked dish-cloth. He was saying, according to the words that floated, in a helium balloon, over his head: *'Now then, men. Pull yourselves together. Time to go to the Bring and Buy sale.'*

The last poster showed Mr and Mrs Waley being held at bay in the street by a giant tarantula that had crept out of a crate of bananas, and now stood in a menacing fashion just in the doorway of their shop. It was a very dark and lively-looking spider. Beneath it, Ione had printed carefully: *You'd be much safer down at our Bring and Buy sale.*

Ned handed the last poster back.

'You are a constant source of surprise for me, Ione,' he told her. 'And yet your father seems quite normal. I wonder what your mother was like.'

'Dad says she was a bit of a sphinx,' said Ione.

Ned grinned.

'There you are, then,' he said.

Ione rolled her eight posters up into a thick roll, snapping on a thick blue elastic band. 'My mother,' she told him proudly, 'could juggle with five balls and ride a unicycle perfectly.'

'I can certainly see why your father took to her,' said Ned Hump.

'The unicycle is still in the toolshed,' said Ione, and leaving the kitchen, she went to find everything she needed to put up her posters.

That evening, Ned and Caroline were disturbed at an early supper, the first one they had shared since the quarrel, by a furious banging on their door.

Caroline rose carefully from the table. Her

freshly washed hair was swathed, none too securely, in a fluffy towel with ducklings all over it. Ned had cooked them both mackerel, and though she knew she looked most odd, she was determined not to let the fishy smell near her hair, in case she had to rinse it again. The yellow duckling towel, for all that it made her look silly, was the only one thick enough for the job. All their other towels had been stolen by Ned's great-aunt from seaside hotels, and were threadbare and half-sized.

The banging on the door got louder and louder.

Caroline jerked the handle and pulled the door open over the warp in the floorboards. As she did so, Ione rushed through like a small tornado, knocking over the cat's water dish and completely ignoring Caroline. Astonished, Caroline flattened herself against the wall, out of harm's way, her turban awry.

'Good gracious,' she said to herself. 'How *rude*.'

She stood watching in growing consternation as Ione, who had flung herself on Ned, sobbed and sobbed, broke off for a moment to say a couple of incomprehensible words, then fell back to sobbing again.

All the time, Ned held her close, and patted

her back, and stroked her hair, and brushed the tears from her cheeks. 'There, there,' he murmured again and again in her ear, looking over her shoulder at Caroline in absolute horror. He'd never seen Ione in this state before.

It was a long time before she calmed down, and longer still before she could stop crying. Ned pushed her down into one of the deep, worn fire-side chairs, and held her hands when she wasn't busy blowing her nose. He peered into her anguished face, and tried to wait till she could tell him of her own accord just what had brought on this tempest of feeling.

But each time Ione dried her eyes, took a deep breath and began to explain, the tears would well up, unbidden, and she would find herself unable to speak again. Ned, kneeling by her side with his arm around her shoulders, would hold her and squeeze her and calm her down again with pats and murmurs and whispers. And Caroline shrank back further and further against the doorpost, appalled. She couldn't imagine what had happened to upset Ione so.

She didn't want to imagine either. She could hardly bear to watch. Indeed, deep inside, she wished Ione had not come rushing in on them with her problem, whatever it was. Caroline felt so uncomfortable. She wished Ione would go and find somebody else to cry on. Why hadn't she gone to her father? It was his job to comfort Ione, not theirs. Not hers. Not Ned's. Ione wasn't *their* daughter, after all. She was pretty nearly grown up, in fact.

Caroline thought it was a bit of a nerve, really, bursting in on them, almost knocking her down, and flinging herself on top of Ned like that, as if she owned him. As if *she* were his wife, and not Caroline.

Ione had been getting on her nerves quite a bit these last few days, now she came to think about it. Ned had been spending far too much time with her, fussing around cheerfully with all the plans for this silly Bring and Buy sale when he should have been wallowing in unhappiness about their stupid quarrel, just as she had been. Ione's sale was no concern of Ned's. What did Ned care about posters and bullocks and hungry people? Those places weren't *their* problem, after all. They were pretty well as far away as they could be. Caroline wanted Ned to care for her; but by the time he'd finished spreading himself out between people who needed seeds and clean water and measles vaccinations, and people who needed their tears wiping away, there was practically no time left over to end this nasty quarrel that had been dragging on for days.

Over Ione's bent head, Ned, still quite baffled, tried to catch Caroline's eye. She shrugged her shoulders at him, cold and indifferent. For a moment, an expression of disappointment showed in Ned's face; and then, just as if he'd dismissed it by force, it disappeared. He turned Ione's tear-swollen face towards him, his own face full of concern.

Caroline felt chilled to the bone. She felt as if her world had shifted slightly and left her un-protected. She had been feeling horrid all week: unsure-of-herself horrid, which she wasn't at all used to and which she now saw was the very worst kind. It hadn't started with the hair-plaiting, either. It had really started hours before that, when Professor Muffet was talking about there being more to living than just sitting around letting life slide past you.

And especially when he had added: 'Surely even *you* can see that.'

That had really upset Caroline. She'd thought about it all morning. She'd still been thinking about it while she was plaiting Ned's hair so tightly into her own. And afterwards she hadn't been able to get it out of her mind all through the angry, quarrelling silences, even when she was sitting doing something she usually found soothing, like brushing her long hair or painting her nails. The idea had kept coming back to make her feel more and more uneasy.

Suppose Professor Muffet were right?

As she stood back in the doorway watching Ned calm Ione, Caroline tried to face for the very first time what it was that had been bothering her. And as soon as she tried, it was easy. She knew at once that there were choices to be made, and she had to make them now and the way that she chose would alter things for ever. Maybe it wasn't enough for her to care only about herself and Ned any longer. Maybe she too should spread herself out a bit.

And she could start right now. After all, here was a perfect opportunity. She could carry on feeling a tiny bit jealous of Ned's love and concern for Ione. Or she could feel ashamed for her own lack of it.

And in a moment the battle within her was over. She felt deeply ashamed of herself. She hung down her head and burst into tears.

'Oh, *Lord*,' Ned groaned. 'Not *another* one.'

He let go of Ione and came over to fetch her. Patting her on the back and nuzzling her under the ears, he led her over to the fireside and pushed her down in the other chair. Then he slipped off to get a bottle of beer from the cache he had spotted earlier at the back of the fridge.

Coming back, he said loudly to both of them: 'That's enough!'

They looked up, startled, just in time to see him flip off the bottle cap and get drenched by burgeoning beer froth.

'I'm so sorry,' said Caroline through her tears. 'I felt mean about not helping you with all those exam papers. I got you some beer for a treat. But then I walked home very fast to give them to you and they must have got all shaken up. I'm so sorry.'

Ned sat on the stool, defeated, soaked and glistening. After a moment's thought, Caroline unravelled her towel and passed it to him so that he could wipe his face. Her own hair fell in damp rats' tails around her tear-stained face, and she caught sight of her reflection in the mirror.

She giggled. After a moment, Ione smiled as well. Caroline did look odd, all straggly and bedraggled. She usually appeared so very neat and cared for. And Ned, for all that he'd wiped his face, still had froth on the rest of him. Tiny bubbles were popping, one after another, on his ears. Ned was, in fact, quietly fizzing. He sounded rather like a soda bottle left open at a picnic.

Ione giggled.

Ned said sternly, 'Are you going to tell us what all this is about? Or did you just pop in for a bit of a cry and a good laugh?'

Ione blushed.

'It *was* dreadful,' she said. 'Truly it was. But it doesn't seem quite so bad now.'

'Tell all,' said Ned, stretching back on the rug at their feet, and balancing his beer bottle on his stomach. 'Take your time. Feel free to go into details, however insignificant they may appear to you. No rush. My secretary here will take notes.'

Caroline stretched out a foot to kick him, but he saw it coming and caught it. He planted it against his stomach, alongside the swaying bottle of beer, and she took to tickling his ribs quietly and gently with her toes. It was the first time they had touched one another in a week.

Ione told all.

Chapter 16

Straight after lunch, Ione had packed up her posters safely in a huge plastic bag. She put two rolls of sticky tape, a pair of scissors, a hammer and a tin of used, mostly bent, tacks into her school bag, and set off to put up the posters of which she was so proud.

She was extremely careful. She tacked the one for her own garden fence to the slats on the corner, under the overhanging yew tree – three tacks on each side. She knew that most of the villagers would walk past it on the way to the shop, and if it did rain, the poster would keep dry there.

She used sticky tape to fix the next to the pillar box. Even before she had finished, a couple of people hurrying up to catch the post had admired it enormously.

The man from the main post office in Eveling

drove up in his van just as she was leaving. He eyed it dubiously.

'Bit cheeky, isn't it?' he asked her, tipping envelopes briskly into his sack, and narrowing his eyes at the little illustration in front of him. 'This isn't a public billboard, you know.'

But when she explained to him exactly what the Very Worthy Cause mentioned on the poster was, he agreed to turn a blind eye until the day after the sale. 'No skin off *my* nose,' he told her cheerfully enough, and she agreed that it wasn't.

Mr Hooper had greeted his poster with cries of delight.

'Splendid!' he told her. 'Lovely! You've drawn a perfect lower central incisor. I *love* that dark shading. That's just a typical example of the plaque people will get if they don't brush, brush, *brush*.' He prowled excitedly around his waiting room. 'Where shall I put it?' he said. 'Let me see . . . I know. Up there by the enlargements of dental caries. Everyone stares at that wall longest.'

Ione handed him four of the least bent tacks and the hammer, and he pounded fiercely on the wall, next to the photographs of blackened rotting teeth and above the shelf of *Miffy* books. Little white flakes of plaster floated down from the mouldings in the ceiling overhead and settled on his bald patch. Ione smiled.

Mr Hooper stepped back to admire her poster once again. 'What a good idea!' he said. 'A Bring and Buy sale! We haven't had one since the Brownies went to Florence. I hope my young patients go and spend all their pocket money on second-hand toys and horrible plastic monsters. Then they won't be able to afford sweets for a week or two. They'll have to steal turnips from Ermyntrude Naseby's allotment if they get hungry in between meals. Do their teeth the world of good.'

'You've got a real thing about turnips, haven't you, Mr Hooper?' Ione observed pleasantly.

Mr Hooper thought about it, leaning against one of his waiting-room chairs, hammer in hand.

'I suppose you're right,' he said finally. 'I suppose I have. But I'm not ashamed of it. Most of the people I've admired have had a thing about something. Why, your own mother had a thing about trees.'

'Trees?'

Ione's eyes widened. She'd known about the unicycling and the juggling. But no one had ever mentioned trees.

'Planting them,' Mr Hooper explained. 'All over. She must have planted hundreds around here. Every time I saw her coming back from a walk with your father, her hands would be caked with mud. She was just as bad before she got married. Nurse Khan swears that on the morning of her wedding she had her little red tin trowel in her bag and chestnut seedlings in her pockets. And the Waleys tell the story of how they bumped into her the day she got back from the honeymoon and asked how the trip was, and her eyes lit up and she told them: 'Better than I could ever have *dreamed*. We planted acorns all over. All over!'

Smiling, he drew Ione over to the window, and pointed to the short cut that ran between Ione's house and the graveyard. 'You see all the young horse chestnuts along that path? Well, your mother planted all those. It was years before she managed to get them all to take. She used to grumble about the gaps constantly whenever she came for a check-up. I thought she meant gaps in her teeth at first, until I realized. I could hardly get into her mouth sometimes, for all her going on. I suppose she would walk down the short cut to get here and it would remind her.'

'I didn't know any of that,' said Ione. 'I didn't even know you did my mother's teeth.'

But Mr Hooper wasn't listening. He was still following his former train of thought.

'After your mother died,' he said, 'your father developed a thing, too. It was about you. Nearly drove us all mad, he did. "Are her eyes straight? Has she got enough hair? Are her feet all right? Does she crawl the way she's supposed to? Shouldn't she be talking by now?" Oh, he was dreadful. He just couldn't be stopped. They sent him home from the cricket tea one Sunday, an hour before it ended, he was boring everyone so. They took a vote on it first, I remember. I was the only one who voted for him, and that was only because I was having a hard time building up my practice then, and couldn't afford to offend him.'

He widened his eyes and stared into space. Ione realized he was miles away, years away.

'Not that he could see me voting for him anyhow,' Mr Hooper rambled on. 'Being blind. And I might have lost a lot of goodwill among the others.' He looked down at his feet and rubbed the fray of one of his laces with the shoe of the other foot. 'But you were a sweet little baby, even with that nasty rash, so I didn't mind voting for him.'

He looked at Ione, wondering.

'That was all a long time ago,' he said. 'A long, long time ago. You didn't have any teeth then. Now look at you. Having your bicuspids extracted. How time flies.'

'Goodbye, then,' said Ione, on the doorstep.

'Goodbye,' said Mr Hooper.

Ione walked on towards the pub, tacking the poster for the church up on the graveyard gate, and the poster for the bus stop up beside the timetable in the shelter.

At the pub doors she stopped and knocked. After a few moments the landlord poked his head out of an upstairs window. 'Not now, Ione,' he told her. 'Arsenal's losing badly. Come back later.'

'Can I stick a poster on your door?' Ione shouted. 'It's for a worthy cause.'

'As long as the worthy cause isn't Temperance!' the landlord shouted back, slamming down the sash window to cut off his bellow of amusement.

Ione unrolled her poster and studied it. She wasn't sure exactly what Temperance was, but she was sure it wasn't bullocks and water pumps, so she stuck the poster firmly on the door with sticky tape. She switched her bag to the other shoulder. The hammer was really heavy, and she was tired. The afternoon seemed to be going by very fast, and she still had two posters.

She walked across the road to the school. She'd hoped it would still be locked up for the holidays, and she could just fasten her poster on the gates without asking Mrs Tallentire's permission. Ione had never been at ease with Mrs Tallentire, and had only been back in the school once since she had left, to see the production of *Dracula* which the Brownies put on six nights in a row to raise funds for their trip to the Dordogne. But the tell-tale green car was parked outside, and the side gate was open. The summer holidays were clearly ending for the primary children. If Mrs Tallentire was back today, they would be back tomorrow, and Ione herself would be next.

Sighing, she walked across the playground and rang the bell.

It seemed an age before Mrs Tallentire came to the entrance hall, carrying a box full of old paper, and opened the door to her.

'Please can I put this poster up on the playground gates?' Ione asked her politely.

'May I,' corrected Mrs Tallentire promptly.

Ione sighed. She found May-I grown-ups trying. It was, she recalled, one of the reasons she had never been at ease with Mrs Tallentire.

'*May* I, then?' she asked.

'I don't think so, Ione,' said Mrs Tallentire. 'The playground gates were not really designed for posters.'

'It's a very worthy cause,' said Ione. 'It's for inoculations and wells and seeds and fishing nets, and things for hungry people.'

As she spoke, she had a sudden blinding image of the other, darker Ned. He was sitting on his heels on the edge of his land, head in hands, rocking his body slowly from side to side. A sense of panic gripped Ione. She could see that he was getting desperate.

'A very worthy cause,' she repeated.

'I'm afraid it might set a bit of a precedent,' said Mrs Tallentire.

'Precedent?'

'All manner of people, seeing your poster, might come wanting to put up posters as well.'

'So?' said Ione.

Mrs Tallentire studied Ione's face closely.

'Are you being insolent, Ione?' she asked.

'No, Mrs Tallentire,' said Ione, falling back

promptly on the dumb, bland tone of voice she knew from experience was the only one Mrs Tallentire could take. 'I'm not, really.'

'The gate's not a noticeboard,' said the head-mistress. 'I'm afraid I can't help you. But if you're going back through it, could you please drop this box beside the wheelie bin for me?'

Ione stood perfectly still for a moment. She was willing every part of her not to feel five years old again, or act that way. And as soon as she was sure she was quite ready, she said calmly:

'I'd better not. After all, it might set a pre-cedent. All manner of people might see and want me to carry things for them.'

She walked out. With immense self-control she pulled the door closed behind her, as quietly as she could. Even if the Brownies put on *Frankenstein* with real forked lightning next year, they would never get her inside the primary school again.

She ought to have stopped right then, she knew. She realized she was getting in a state. But the shop was on the way home, and this was an important poster. Everybody in the village shopped at Waley's.

Ione pushed open the door. Above her head

the buzzer rang, and Mr Waley looked round. He held his little grandson Geoffrey in one crooked arm, and with the other he was stacking bags of flour one by one onto a shelf.

Geoffrey was grizzling softly, and didn't stop when Ione smiled at him.

'Please will you put this poster up in your window?' she asked.

'I don't take posters, Ione,' Mr Waley said. 'They cut out the light.'

'But I made it for you specially,' she told him, slipping the bag off her shoulder onto the floor and unrolling the poster to show him. 'It's for a worthy cause and it will only have to be up for a week.'

'I don't take posters,' he repeated.

'Please,' she pleaded.

She was beginning to feel queasy, and her voice trembled slightly. 'It's to help people in some of the poorest places in the world.'

'I've got my own worries at the moment, thank you, Ione,' Mr Waley said, shifting Geoffrey from one arm to the other.

'But these people are going hungry,' Ione said, close to tears. 'Starving.'

'I'm sure they could manage a whole lot better

if they tried a little harder themselves,' said Mr Waley. 'A lot of them waste their time and effort fighting one another, then expect us to organize help when things get desperate. Besides, there's so much thieving and waste that most of what's sent probably never even gets there.'

He put Geoffrey down on the counter. But Geoffrey immediately began to scream, and Mr Waley was forced to pick him up again almost at once.

Ione tried to stay calm.

'There's bound to be a bit of waste if they're in trouble,' she told him. 'It's hard for a country to be organized at the best of times. And a lot of the problem is that we don't send them the right things. Half the time we end up sending them things that it suits our factories to make: guns and helicopters and bits for fancy airports. If we really wanted to help them properly, we'd send them the things they really need. Rotovators and water pumps and chickens and bullocks. We've decided to buy a bullock with the profit from our Bring and Buy sale. Bullocks are very sturdy animals. They can pull ploughs and water up out of wells, and you can even breed them to get more. In some places they even turn out to be more useful than tractors.'

Mr Waley jammed the last of the bags of flour onto the shelf and shifted Geoffrey back to the other arm. He'd had a very bad day. Geoffrey was missing his parents, who were away at a wedding. He'd kept him and his wife up all the night before with his crying, and he was probably going to do the same tonight. Geoffrey was teething, and Mr Waley had a headache. He didn't quite know why he was picking an argument with Ione. All he really wanted was for her to go away and leave him in peace, taking her poster with her.

'You don't want to bother with all that,' he told her. 'It's not your problem. Why don't you just run around and enjoy yourself in the last few days of your summer holidays, like a sensible girl? Get a bit of colour in your cheeks. If there's that many of them who need help, one bullock isn't going to do much good, is it?'

'It would help quite a few people,' Ione argued. 'Several families could share it. They're better at sharing things than some of us are.'

She looked at him meaningfully over the counter.

Mr Waley became irritated with Ione. He stepped out from behind the scales and began to steer her towards the door. But Geoffrey started to bellow and, losing his patience, Mr Waley turned on Ione instead.

'Off you go,' he snapped. 'Out of the shop, please, and take your poster with you. You're as bad as your mother, you are, with all your notions. She seemed to think she could turn the whole country back into a forest, and you think you can feed the world. Go on. Off you go. Go on home now.'

Ione shook herself free. She turned to face him, her eyes wide with fury. All the blood left her cheeks. She looked very much older suddenly, and very, very pale.

'I'm *proud* of my mother,' she said in a voice so choked with anger that he hardly would have recognized it as hers, 'whatever *you* say about her. And I feel sorry for Geoffrey. Because if you were *my* grandfather I would find it very difficult to be proud of *you*. And I shall never, never, *ever* shop here again.'

'*Good*,' said Mr Waley, and he slammed the door behind her.

Chapter 17

She had run home, enraged as never before. She hurtled through the front door and collided with her father, who was rooting around, trying to find a shopping bag. It was time for Mandy's walk and Professor Muffet wanted to pick up a few groceries from Mr Waley on the way back.

'You can't shop there any more,' Ione told him, breathless from her run home.

She told him what had happened.

Ione's father listened to her jumbled account of the afternoon with a serious expression on his face. As soon as she'd finished he began pacing up and down the hall rug, looking very unhappy. Ione wondered if he were fretting about where they would buy their last-minute groceries in future. Till now she hadn't given that any thought herself. But she saw with a sinking feeling that his face was set graver than for a worry like that.

He stopped his pacing and stood in front of her.

'You will have to go back and apologize,' he said.

Ione was astonished. Hadn't he been listening properly? Hadn't he understood? He knew how important the Bring and Buy sale was to her now. She'd told him all about the posters and the helium balloons over supper. He'd seemed really pleased about it. Delighted, in fact.

And now he had turned on her, just like that, without a word of warning. Ione was bitterly hurt, and very angry. After all, it was he who had gone on to Caroline about Ione not doing things. He hadn't realized she'd been listening, of course, but that was beside the point. He'd let her down. Worse than that, not only had he wanted her to do things, but he expected her to go out again to apologize for doing them. It was so unfair.

'You'll have to say you're sorry,' he said again.

Ione sat down hard on the bottom stair and stamped her feet wildly.

'Why *should* I?' she shouted. 'Why *should* I? He's a *pig*. He's thoughtless and selfish and *rude*. He'd let Ned Hump starve to death right in front of his eyes. He was *hateful*. I *hate* him. I'll *never* go in there again. I'd rather die than apologize to *him*.'

'You *have* to apologize,' Professor Muffet said simply. 'You have no choice.' He sat beside his daughter on the stairs and took her hand. It shook with anger and felt soft and cold. He squeezed it several times, but Ione was far too upset to respond.

'Listen,' he said to her when he thought he'd allowed her sufficient time to calm down. 'You're being unfair to Mr Waley. He wouldn't let Ned starve to death in front of his eyes – or anybody else for that matter – you know he wouldn't.'

'Why won't he help me get my bullock, then?'

'Because he doesn't see the link between the two as clearly as you do, that's why. He isn't cruel. He's just not as wrapped up in it all as you are. If everyone had a thing about raising money to send aid where it's needed, no one would ever sculpt or paint or even learn to ride a unicycle. They'd all be out doing sponsored parachute jumps and running Oxfam shops.'

'I suppose so,' said Ione ruefully. 'But I still don't see why I have to say I'm sorry to him. He was far ruder than I was.'

'He may have been ruder to you than you were to him,' said Professor Muffet, 'but you hurt him much, much more. You said that if he was your grandfather, you wouldn't be proud of him. That's an awful thing to say. He must be feeling dreadful now. You could hardly have chosen anything more devastating to say.' He squeezed her hand again. 'So, you see,' he said. 'You have to go back. You have to go and tell him you were wrong.'

'I wasn't wrong,' said Ione. 'If he was my grandfather, I wouldn't be proud of him. And I'm not going.'

Professor Muffet let go of her hand. He stood up. He could see he was getting nowhere with her. She was as stubborn as her mother.

'Ione,' he said, 'I'm giving you till breakfast time tomorrow to think of one nice thing about Mr Waley that a granddaughter of his could be proud of. And till lunchtime to tell him you're sorry. And if you can't tell me by then that you've tried to make peace with Mr Waley, then you can just cancel your Bring and Buy sale. Because, if by doing some good for people you don't know, you just end up hurting and despising those you do, then you'd better not do any good at all. You'd better wait a few years till you're old enough either to do something useful without making enemies, or not to mind seeing the people you antagonize cross the street when they see you coming.'

Ione stared at him. She was so taken aback she couldn't speak. First he wanted her to do things, then he threatened to stop her. Wouldn't she *ever* get things right? She opened her mouth a couple of times to argue, but she couldn't think of anything to say.

Suddenly the whole day flooded in on her: the hours she had spent on the posters; the time she had spent putting them up; all that talk about her mother; Mrs Tallentire's niggliness; her row with Mr Waley; and now her own father was against her, or so it seemed. If this was what came of listening to other people talk about you, then she would have no more of it. She would never eavesdrop again.

'Well?' he asked sternly. 'Well?'

Tears pricked behind Ione's eyes and she clenched her fists till the knuckles paled. She was ready to fly at him. She wanted to hit him, hard. He wouldn't see it coming and he could never hit her back.

Ione made for the door as fast as she could. She

ran off, out across the lawn towards the gate. She left the front door swinging.

Professor Muffet felt the draught but he did not move to close the door. Instead he sat down on the bottom stair again and put his head in his hands.

As soon as she was sure that the shouting was over, Mandy crept out from where she had been hiding, deep in the hall cupboard. She wriggled close and licked Professor Muffet's fingers wetly; but he was feeling far too shaken to respond.

'He was right, you know,' said Ned, lying flat on his back on the rug. 'Maddening as it may be to you, young, passionate and idealistic as you are, he's perfectly right.'

Ned was becoming expansive, Ione noticed. It had taken her some time to tell everything and he was well down the bottle of beer.

'If he were to let you get away with it,' Ned went on, 'you'd turn into a prig. It's the major pitfall for people who have worthy causes. An awful lot of them fall in it.'

'You don't fall in a pitfall,' quibbled Caroline. 'A pitfall falls on you.'

Ione smiled. She didn't mind Caroline's

niggling. It was a whole lot different from Mrs Tallentire's. And Ione felt much happier now. She realized that none of it seemed so bad any more. Not everything was as spoiled as she'd believed. She could see she had been horrid to poor Mr Waley. She could even imagine making friends with him again, if he would let her.

'Next thing you know,' Ned said, waving his bottle around in the air, 'you'll despise all of us. Your father for writing Useless Old History Books About Food Riots that will never feed anyone; me for not being able to read anyone's writing; and Caroline for being totally indifferent to the world's ills just so long as her nails are beautifully polished and her hair is perfection.'

Caroline blushed. Her nails were, indeed, beautifully polished, but she had made a lot of decisions in the last hour. It would have been hard for anyone to listen to Ione's tale without being impressed by her determination. And Caroline had been very impressed indeed. Ione had never been at all like that before. If someone like Ione could suddenly just show a whole other side of herself that no one had ever suspected was there, maybe Caroline could too.

Caroline didn't mind Ned's teasing. She might

even slip off and sort her hair out in a while. But she would surprise Ned in the long run. Ned would see.

Ione slid out of the armchair. 'I'd better go home now,' she said. 'And thank you both very much.'

'You're welcome,' said Ned. 'Any time you feel like a bit of sobbing and raving and giggling, you're to drop in, isn't she, Caroline?'

Caroline didn't answer. She was absorbed, trying to brush out all the knots that had dried in her long silky hair.

Ione walked slowly home in the gathering dark. There was nobody about. It must be pretty late, she thought to herself. She was tired out.

She could hear, from further along the street, a rattling of keys. Just at that moment, a lamp was switched on in one of the cottages, lighting up part of the pavement. She saw Mr Waley there, outside his shop, his keys in his hand. And as she drew nearer, under the street lamp, he saw her too.

He started. Then he continued to look in her direction, but gave no further sign that he had seen her. His face was closed and expressionless.

Casually, he began whistling softly to himself.
And though his house, Ione knew, was in the
direction she herself was coming from, and he
ought really to walk past her, instead he walked
hurriedly across the street away from her, and disappeared down an alley that ran between the post
office and the cottages.

It was a long time before Ione fell asleep that
night. And by the time Mr Waley came to open
up his shop at half-past eight the following morning, she had already been waiting for him for
twenty minutes.

Chapter 18

On Thursday night it rained. Ione was woken by the noise of it, splattering and beating against the panes of glass above her head, sheeting off the blocked and rusted gutters outside her window like syrup off a giant spoon, and falling in heavy uneven splashes onto the flooded paths below. The rain-soaked branches of the prunus leaned so far over that they tapped the sodden house walls; and the ill-fitting lid on the garden water-butt below began to thud gently and rhythmically as the rising wind lifted it and then let it fall, over and over.

Ione lay on her back, with her arms crooked under her head, staring up at the ceiling through the darkness. It's been a long time, she told herself happily. A very long time.

She was filled with the most enormous sense of

relief. The long, long summer was over. The sheer wetness of everything would drive it away within hours. The ground would soften, the grass would turn green once again, and the shrubbery leaves would glisten, dark and fresh, in the morning.

'The rains,' she whispered softly to herself, half in returning sleep. 'Here come the rains.'

Straight after breakfast Ned came round for Ione. They were going out to collect bric-a-brac together.

He stood in the steadily pouring rain, in a large puddle, looking quite extraordinary even for him, and he wasn't known in the village as a natty dresser. He had on a huge flapping bicycle cape made from shiny black rubber, so loose and long that it looked rather as if he had chosen to deck himself out for the day in a smallish tent. Its capacious hood covered his head and most of his face, making him appear strangely sinister, like a lanky grave-digger, or one of Dracula's more secretive henchmen. In one hand he carried a cracked and rusting old hand-bell, and in the other a length of frayed rope which trailed round the corner, and at which he tugged fruitlessly from time to time.

'What have you got at the end of that rope?' Ione asked him, staying safe under the porch while she zipped her waterproof jacket right up to her chin, and pulled her rainhat on tightly.

'My hand-cart,' said Ned. 'We need a cart. We can't be forever trudging to and from the church hall with small armfuls. We are going to be efficient about this bric-a-brac collecting.' He hitched his hood up even further over his face till only his mouth and chin could be seen. 'We are going to boil down what has been treated hithertofore as an inept art into one of the more exact sciences.' He opened the gate for her courteously, and then nearly ran her down with his little wooden wagon. 'I intend to write a short paper on my findings, to be published in *Science Quarterly*. I think I may break new ground.'

'I think you have already,' said Ione, looking behind her. 'Your cart's wheels have shredded our lawn.'

'Sorry,' said Ned.

They began at the east end of the village street, according to a plan that Ned had conceived while shaving.

Ned took the lead. He hauled along the cart by the rope that went over his shoulder, stooping more than usual, and limping and hobbling horribly, and ending each stride with a shudder, frightful to look at.

'What on earth are you doing?' asked Ione.

'Trust me,' said Ned, over his shoulder. 'Just trust me. We've only got till Saturday. If we do it your way, the normal way – "Please can we have something for our Bring and Buy sale, ma'am?" – all we'll end up with is two broken fish-slices and a lot of promises. So keep quiet and trust me.'

He staggered along the dripping, glistening street, splashing through the puddles, and as he went, he tolled his bell slowly and sonorously.

'Bring out your dead!' he shouted through the steady rain in a forced cracked voice with an odd rustic accent. 'Bring 'em out, people. Bring out your dead!'

He kept it up all the way along the street – the cart rumbling along loudly in his wake – and half of the way back.

After a while, Ione noticed that several of the lace curtains in the cottage windows had begun to twitch. Curious faces appeared at the upstairs windows of the larger houses, and parents with toddlers beside them or babies on their hips sidled noiselessly into half-opened doorways.

'Bring out your dead!' bellowed Ned, even more loudly. 'Come on. Can't leave 'em rotting. Bring 'em all out!'

Suddenly a bedroom window just above him opened up with a piercing creak.

'Is that you, Ned Hump?' shouted Nurse Khan, leaning out dangerously far.

'Bain't be no Ned 'Ump around 'ere what I know of,' Ned bellowed back up at her. 'There were one Lord Edward 'Ump, and a fine, strapping, handsome, charming, intelligent lad he were, to be sure. A joy to 'is family and a credit to the county. But 'e's been dead and gone a week or more. Why, I took 'is fair young body away to the pits myself, on this very cart. 'E was one of the first to go.' He shook his head sadly from side to side, and waggled a finger at Nurse Khan. 'It's always the cream as gets skimmed off first, so they do say.'

Nurse Khan stared down at him, speechless.

More doors opened. More pairs of eyes stared. Ione was torn between blushing and giggling. In the end, she did both.

'What *is* he doing?' someone shouted from away down the street. 'Is that Ned Hump? What on earth does he *want*?'

'What do you want?' someone closer shouted at Ned.

'Your dead,' said Ned, as he limped and hobbled back down the street. 'Bring out your dead!'

'You'll get no sense out of *him*,' said Nurse Khan. 'He's a right loon. Ask Ione. Ione, whatever is he up to? What does he want?'

'Stuff to sell,' said Ione, pulling herself together fast, and speaking as clearly as she could through tears of laughter. 'He's collecting bric-a-brac. He wants it for Saturday's Bring and Buy sale.'

'Oh, for heaven's *sake*!' said Nurse Khan, totally exasperated, and she slammed the bedroom window shut.

Ned parked the cart in the middle of the street, halfway from each end, and waited, tolling his bell.

Sure enough, his scheme had worked. He had caught the whole street's attention within minutes. One by one, the doors opened wider, and the things began to pour out.

Ned and Ione ran here and there, up and down the street, from one side of the road to the other, from door to door, taking the proffered goods in armfuls, bringing them back to the cart and slipping them under the tarpaulin Ned had left on the top, to keep everything dry.

They were given egg-cups in sets of three, armfuls of magazines, children's outgrown clothes, discarded bedspreads and even a set of matching birdcages.

'I was going to sell them at the next car boot sale,' said Mr Priestley. 'But since they're cluttering up the hallway, and you're *here* . . .'

They were given eighteen pounds of chutney in large jars. 'Too hot for us, love,' said the lady who pressed the carton on them. 'Sell it as curry paste I should, if I were you.'

Ned struggled under the weight of a handloom in several heavy pieces which he felt obliged to carry to the cart for Ione.

'My daughter was going to sell it on e-bay,' Mrs Orion told them. 'But she's been so very busy.'

Ione trapped her finger in a large toy garage, and stained the front of her jacket with some uncapped yellow ochre from a box of ancient oil colours. She counted four sieves, nearly a dozen broken fish-slices, and scores of paperbacks.

'All this stuff,' she breathed, marvelling at the amount and the variety. 'All this *stuff.*'

And on the door of every house from which

237

they had been handed something, Ned chalked a large cross.

'I suppose you think that's very funny indeed,' said the choirmaster's wife, who used to teach history, and now ran a Chronic Family Sickness Support Group.

Within ten minutes, every door on the street where someone had been home bore the tell-tale mark of generosity.

'Tell all your neighbours who are out at work,' said Ned, 'that we'll be back this evening.' He turned to Ione. 'Come along,' he said.

Just at that moment a curtain in front of them twitched.

Ned froze. Then, as the rest of the street watched from doorsteps or windowsills or from behind their curtains, he bore down on this one door with his noisy cart and his noisy bell.

He planted himself just before the doorstep, and rapped the knocker, long and loud.

'Come on out, you old bat,' he shouted. 'Show your face and hand over your jumble.'

The door opened a crack.

'You go away, Ned Hump,' came a high, spirited voice. 'You go away and boil your head.'

Ned clanged his bell furiously.

'If you don't hand over some jumble before I count to twenty,' he yelled, 'I'm going to write a *very rude word* on your nice door in my fluorescent, indelible chalk. And you'd better start jumble-hunting right now, you mean-spirited old bat, because I'm starting to count.'

He began counting aloud, slowly and menacingly.

The whole street waited, breathless with excitement.

He had reached seventeen before the door opened again, just halfway, and Ermyntrude Naseby hobbled out onto her doorstep, wagging her head wildly from side to side, and waving a coal shovel threateningly in Ned's direction.

'Lovely,' said Ned, reaching out for it. 'Very nice. Most acceptable. Hand it over.'

'You keep off, Ned Hump,' croaked Ermyntrude Naseby, livid with rage. 'This is to hit you with, not to give you.'

'Come on, you old troll,' Ned wheedled. 'What's a bit of old bric-a-brac going to set you back? One cluttered cupboard, that's all. Come on. Listen, I'll be reasonable. I'm not after anything fancy. I'll settle for two torn antimacassars and a plastic doily.'

239

'I haven't got any bric-a-brac,' the old lady insisted in her cracked, penetrating voice. 'And even if I did have, I'd die rather than give any of it to the likes of you.'

'You'll have to make biscuits, then,' said Ned, 'for the food stall.'

She stared at him, horrified, completely taken aback. Her mouth dropped open.

'Biscuits?' she whispered. '*Me?*'

'Yes,' said Ned firmly. 'It's up to you. There are going to be no free-loaders at Saturday's sale. It's called a Bring and Buy sale. And I'm not going to let you come and *buy* if you haven't *brought*. So it's either something to sell or home-made biscuits, or you can't come.'

A tremor of horror ran down the street. Ione could hear it, like a chill, fast breath.

'Can't come? *Can't come?*'

'That's right,' Ned repeated. 'We won't let you come. We'll throw you out. You won't be allowed to so much as finger the cracked plates. If you won't contribute then you can't come round on Saturday, scavenging off the rest of us busy citizenry. Being eighty-eight is no excuse at all. None. The same rules go for you as for the rest of us. No bring, no buy, and that's that.'

There was dead silence for several moments.

It was so quiet, each raindrop seemed to make an audible splash. The people watched and waited, waited and watched, spellbound.

Ned shrank inside his cloak, as he too waited. Ermyntrude Naseby stood perfectly still.

Then, without warning, she turned on her heel and disappeared back into her house, leaving the door ajar.

Not a soul spoke. Even the babies were quiet.

Within a minute she was back. She appeared on her doorstep like a witch in a fury. She flung a complete set of plastic measuring spoons at Ned's head, catching him on the ear, and then tossed a large darned tablecloth and several stained napkins onto the cart. Then she went back inside, slamming the door viciously behind her.

Ned turned and picked up the plastic measuring spoons. He wiped the mud off them with his fingers and handed them to Ione, who put them neatly in a teapot on the top of the cart. Then, as loud, ringing applause broke out from every open doorway in the street, Ned bowed low, two or three times.

'Come along, Ione,' he said. 'We are falling rather badly behind our schedule.'

She followed him, as he limped and stooped down the wet street, tolling his bell, and shouting, 'Bring out your dead!'

The applause lasted until they had turned the corner.

Here, Ned turned to her, and pushed the hood back off his face for a moment.

'See?' he said to her proudly. '*See?*'

Chapter 19

They worked all morning without a break, collecting stuff to sell. Each time the cart filled to overflowing with toasters, gardening tools, plant pots, kettles and old videos, Ned would haul it off to the church hall and tip it in unruly piles on the cloakroom floor.

They would lean against the wall for a while, admiringly, and then trundle the cart back for more. By mid-afternoon they had gathered together an astonishing number of things, and both of them were exhausted.

'It would have been far easier with three,' Ned said at one point, as they staggered to the cart under the weight of a large wooden dog-kennel that Mrs Asprey had kindly donated. 'Caroline should have come with us. She promised yesterday that she would. But when I reminded her this morning, she said she had something more important to do.'

He shook his head forlornly. Sometimes it seemed to him that Caroline always wriggled out of any job, however important it might be, that would make her get cold or wet or scruffy. That was one quality in Ione that he had really come to admire, he reflected. She didn't mind getting cold and wet *and* scruffy.

He peered at her more closely through the rain. She looked far too cold, he thought. Frightfully wet and downright filthy.

'That's it,' he said decisively. 'That's the lot. I'm not doing any more. We'll just take this lot back and then we'll go home.'

Ione pushed her rainhat back a little. Her face was very pale and strained.

'There are only two more streets to do,' she said wistfully.

All through the day, whenever what she was carrying had been heavy and awkward, or had trapped her fingers, whenever she stepped into a puddle that was deeper than she expected, and the water had run over into her shoes, making her socks squelch miserably, whenever the rain forced itself down her neck, or her hands had stiffened from cold, or she had felt the tears of exhaustion and exasperation rise in her eyes, she had brought back in her mind the picture of the other, darker Ned standing on the edge of his wide, hot, barren, lifeless plain, waiting and wondering what on earth he was going to do.

The picture came to mind now, and she stood still, drenched by the rain, absorbed.

'Enough is enough,' said Ned firmly.

He took her hand and led her back towards the church.

The little wooden wagon rumbled and splashed along behind them, as it had all day.

Stuck up in the oak tree that overlooked the school playground, unable to get down again, Caroline heard, above the shouts and yells and screams of the home-going children, the noisy rumble of the cart.

She shifted the huge peppermint she was sucking from one cheek to the other.

Rescue, she thought. At last, I shall be rescued.

She had been stuck up the tree well over an hour, since the children's mid-afternoon break. She was damp, chilled and cramped.

She looked down through the leafy mass of

branches from which she could not descend without help, and saw her husband and Ione coming.

'Ned,' she called out. '*Ned!*'

The peppermint tucked in her cheek made her voice thick and unrecognizable.

'Ned!'

Ned Hump stopped dead in his tracks. Baffled, he stared up – first into the oak tree and then beyond, into the sky.

'Ned,' he heard the strange voice again. 'Ned!'

'Yes, God?' said Ned.

Caroline, from her perch in the tree, saw his blank, staring face.

'I need help, Ned,' she called down to him.

'Anything you say, God,' said Ned, dropping to his knees in the gutter.

Ione gazed up too, dazed with tiredness and surprise.

Caroline, exasperated, spat out her peppermint. It landed just beside the kneeling Ned, shattering into a hundred white fragments.

'Look, Ione,' said Ned. 'A thunderbolt.'

Ione burst out laughing.

The voice that came from above was now entirely recognizable. Irritable, edgy and unmistakably Caroline's: 'Get off your knees this minute, Ned Hump, and stop your fooling. Help me down out of this stupid tree.'

Ned rose to his feet.

'The lady moves in mysterious ways, her wonders to perform,' he observed softly to Ione. Then he stepped under the branches that were shaking and rustling above his head.

From out of the tree, a pair of large red Wellington boots descended slowly.

Ned reached up and seized them. He directed one onto each shoulder.

'Steady,' he warned her. 'Don't let go yet, Sweetpea. Steady.'

'Ned,' hissed Caroline from between clenched teeth. 'I am in no position up here to be choosy.'

Ione watched, fascinated, as Ned began to sway one way, and Caroline's legs, above him, began to sway another.

'Easy,' Ned shouted. 'If you could just slide down *slowly*.'

'*Help!*' shrieked Caroline, panicking. 'Don't drop me, Ned. Hold *on*.'

Ned held on. It was the worst thing he could have done. Caroline wriggled and flailed and thrashed and fought, and as the branches she was depending upon cracked and gave, she fell on top of him and they ended up on the street in a chaotic, muddy heap.

In his right hand, Ned still clutched one of Caroline's boots. He was winded and grazed.

'Oaf!' said Caroline. 'Clumsy oaf.'

'Idiot,' Ned returned fondly. 'What on earth were you *doing* up there?'

Without getting up, for she was far too wet and grubby now for it to make any difference, Caroline dug in her pocket and handed him a paper dart.

Raising his eyebrows, he unfolded it.

It was a photocopied notice, written in easy words and large, round letters:

Come and get a big red helium balloon. Come to the church hall on Saturday at half-past two. Tell your friends. Lots of toys and games. Bring all your pocket money. Don't forget.

Underneath, there was a copy of Ione's drawing of Mrs Tallentire being swept up and away by a crowd of helium balloons.

'I sent dozens of them over,' said Caroline proudly. 'I became really rather skilled at it. I could even hit people who hadn't got one yet. I think almost all of them got one in the end. They had a great time. They chased about after them, making a dreadful din. The biggies read them out to the babies, and explained what helium balloons were. None of them would go in at the end of break, they were so over-excited. They kept running out of line to pick up the spares. Mrs Tallentire had to come out and shriek at them.' Caroline smiled warmly at the memory. 'She went wild. She kept trying to work out where they were coming from, but I was too clever for her.'

She explored a sore place on her cheek gently with her fingers.

'Not clever enough to get down again, though,' she ended forlornly. 'I'm going to get a terrible bruise. I shall be quite disfigured.'

She stood up.

'Can we go home now, Ned?' she asked him plaintively. 'Have you two finished too?' She shivered. 'I've been up there ever since lunchtime and I'm so very cold and wet.'

Ned gazed at her, full of love and admiration. Then he kissed her. She was cold; she was wet; and she was gloriously, gloriously scruffy.

Chapter 20

Saturday morning dawned bright and beautiful. Ione lay in her bed, watching the sunlight sweep across her bedroom wall. Stretching out her toes between the tangled sheets, she let herself bathe in visions of prancing, dancing coins, fluttering ten-pound notes and the occasional signed cheque.

She purred softly. It was going to be a splendid, wonderful day.

Ned got up early and walked over the lawn to the vicarage, interrupting the vicar at his breakfast. The vicar was spooning lemon curd onto his toast and listening to the news on the radio.

'We need the church hall keys,' Ned explained. 'Everything we've collected for our sale is still outside in the cloakroom. We have to get it in and set it all out on the trestle tables by two o'clock.'

The vicar lifted his head. He hated being bothered at breakfast. And Ned had talked right through the price index figures he had wanted to catch.

'Keys?' he said irritably. 'I haven't got the keys. And the church hall is all locked up this weekend. Midway and Sons painted the walls yesterday, and they're coming back on Monday to varnish the woodwork.' He saw Ned's face. 'They *always* take the keys away with them when they paint the church hall. They have done ever since the Brownies got in too early one time to rehearse *Night of the Living Dead,* and covered the walls with fingerprints before the paint dried.'

Ned sat down heavily at the breakfast table.

'Oh,' he said. 'Oh, dear.'

He reached out unthinkingly for the lemon curd pot and dipped his finger in. 'Nice,' he said, licking appreciatively. 'Not too sweet.'

The vicar prised the pot from between Ned's fingers and placed it safely out of reach behind the salt cellar.

'You'll have to postpone the sale,' he said. 'You should never have chosen today in the first place. It's most irregular. You should always ask first. It's my job to arrange all these things, after all,' he added petulantly, wiping his mouth with a paper napkin. 'That's exactly what I'm here for.'

'Is it?' asked Ned, with quickening interest. 'Is it really? I had no idea. I thought you were here for baptisms and weddings and funerals and visiting the sick and suchlike. I thought Bring and Buy sale arrangements and church hall redecorating was just a sideline of yours. I had no idea that was exactly what you were here for.'

The vicar, irritated, rose and pushed his chair in neatly under the table. There was a strong anticlerical streak in Ned Hump, he reflected, that he'd never much cared for.

'You'll have to sort it out yourself,' he said. 'I'm off to a conference. We all are. All the clergy, including the Bishop himself, are meeting at Rutherstrop today to discuss the changes in the tax laws.'

'Heavens above,' said Ned respectfully.

The vicar picked up his car keys and left in a small huff.

Ned pushed the salt aside, retrieved the lemon curd pot, and sat there quietly for a while, spooning curd into his mouth with his finger, thinking.

* * *

Caroline was overtaken by the vicar on the wicked left-hand bend that led into the narrow bridge over Rutherstrop river, where the accident black spot warning sign used to be before the juggernaut ripped it out, jack-knifing into the weir. She wondered why he was in such a hurry. She herself was taking her time, enjoying the passing countryside – considerably fresher since the heavy rain, she thought – and at the steadily rising white mists that presaged a glorious day.

She was driving to Novelties Incorporated & Fairground Supplies. It was hidden away behind the self-storage units and took some time to find.

'I want a helium balloon gas canister thing,' she told the man in the warehouse. 'And hundreds of balloons. And thirty novelties, for prizes.'

The man yawned and scratched at his ear. A pencil that had been wedged behind it fell off, onto the floor. He picked it up and began writing yesterday's date on a bright yellow invoice slip. 'Sweet little bath ducks that float or nasty little skeleton key rings that squirt water in your face?' he asked her, yawning again.

Caroline thought about it.

On the one hand, none of the children she had seen the day before in the playground had looked old enough to have things they had to keep locked. On the other hand, none of them looked that partial to bathing, either.

There again, a lot of the Brownies might come . . .

'Nasty little skeleton key rings that squirt water in your face,' she said.

The man showed her how to fill the balloons from the gas cylinder, and instructed her in a faster and better way to knot them.

'You're going to break every single one of your pretty nails today,' he warned her with gloomy satisfaction.

Caroline looked down at her pink, glistening fingertips.

'Oh, well,' she sighed. 'It's a very worthy cause.'

He helped her load the stuff into the back of the car. 'I'll give you a tip,' he said kindly, just before she drove off. 'A rule of thumb, as it were. If they pop or lose them the minute they get them, give them another free. If they come back later with a sob-story, however convincing, make them pay again. It's the only way.'

'Wise,' said Caroline. 'Very wise. Thank you.'

She drove back to the village, humming.

* * *

Ione pushed open the door of the toolshed. The wood felt soft and damp and half-rotten against her fingertips, and she wrinkled her nose against the thick, musty smell inside.

She was looking for her doll's house. She wanted to give something to the sale, something from her. She had already put a few books and some old jigsaws into a cardboard box; but none of that was worth much. She wanted to give something that would sell for enough to make up a sizeable bit of the bullock, and she knew that her doll's house was the only thing.

It was still there, where she had thought it would be, beside the unicycle in the dark back corner, which the light from the grimy window entirely failed to reach. It was painted white, with a peaked high red roof, and a hinged front. Over the door, there were roses – little fat globules of hard scarlet paint on finely drawn creepers. There were tiny black metal shutters. The windows opened and the door latched. The rooms were small, delicate and beautifully painted. Each of the bedrooms even had a fireplace with a mantelpiece, and the staircase had banisters as delicate as matchsticks.

It was empty of furniture now. Ione had no

idea where all the furniture had gone. It was a long time since she had played with it.

Kneeling, she ran her fingertips over the dust that lay in a thin film over the roof, and she fiddled with the upstairs windows. She did not open it. She wasn't sure that she could give it away if she looked at it too closely. It had been very dear to her once.

As she lifted it off the floor, she heard a clatter from behind, and a tiny red tin trowel fell out from the shelf of a broken bookcase against which the doll's house had been carelessly jammed. It fell at her feet.

Ione put the doll's house down on the hood of the old barbecue and stooped to pick up the little red trowel. She thought back to what Mr Hooper had said about her mother. Holding it tightly in her hand, she wondered.

Then, leaving the door ajar for when she returned to fetch the doll's house, she took the trowel away with her, across the lawn to the summerhouse.

Her papers still lay scattered on the flagstones. A lot of them were wet. Damp patches still darkened the floor after the rain, and the spider had gone from its web.

Ione stood in the middle of her summerhouse, looking around. There was nowhere to put the trowel or the papers. Nowhere. There was nowhere to keep anything. She'd never had anything to keep in there before. She thought she might ask Ned to help her carry in a large box and a table later, when there was more time. She thought they might come in very useful in the future, whenever she was busy with things. But now she just gathered the pamphlets up into a tidy pile and put the little red tin trowel down on the top, to keep them there.

Just as she rose to her feet, a light breeze blew in through the open lattices, rustling the papers softly under the trowel.

Why don't they tell you things? Ione said to herself, as she gently pulled the door closed behind her. Why do you have to hear quite by chance the things you always needed to know?

Chapter 21

By the time Ione reached the churchyard, tugging her doll's house behind her on the little wooden trolley, Ned had been busy for an hour. He had set up at least a third of the stuff to be sold.

Ione stared.

There was bric-a-brac all over the graves. Old garden tools lay neatly against Captain Flook's pillar. Martha Cuddlethwaite's grave was covered in kitchen equipment. The foodstuffs were stacked neatly upon Thomas Morton. The war memorial was knee-deep in soft toys, and baby clothes were draped tastefully from the low hanging branches of the cypresses.

'Come along,' said Ned briskly, hauling a large hairy rug over to the church steps. 'We haven't got all day. I want you to put all the ornaments on Theresa Cunningham while I finish stacking the books on the Hobsons.'

'You *can't*, Ned,' Ione cried out, horrified. 'It's *sacrilege*.'

'Nonsense,' said Ned.

'Heresy, then,' Ione insisted. 'It's something dreadful, anyhow.'

'Rubbish,' said Ned. 'Don't be medieval.' He waved an arm around airily. 'They might as well make themselves useful for once,' he told her. 'They just lie around all day, after all. It'll bring a bit of purpose into their lives. I mean deaths.'

'You're so *bad*,' said Ione. 'I never met anyone who could be as *bad* as you can be when you try.'

But she set to work obediently all the same.

By noon, they had everything almost straight. Caroline had taken over the pricing, sticking neat little white labels on everything in sight. Ione took over the job of guessing what things were, and where they should go, and Ned found a large red tin box to keep the money in.

He strode around the graves looking for somewhere to set up the cash desk.

'Here's a good one,' he called out at last. Ione came over to look. Hidden in the weeds was a flat grave, about the height of a coffee table. Creepers had covered one end, and there was a stain of moss over the surface. But the inscription could still be read quite clearly on its face:

> *Death is a debt to nature due,*
> *Which I have paid, and so must you.*

'Fine,' she told him, pleased. 'Perfect.'

She was getting altogether taken with the idea now, Ned saw.

It came as a surprise to them when Officer Morton interrupted them, shortly after lunchtime. He leaned over the wall, looking hot and cross in his dark blue uniform.

'What's all this?' he said to them. 'What's going on here? You can't do this. You can't hold a sale in a graveyard. The very *idea*!'

They looked at one another silently, each hoping one of the others would explain.

Officer Morton strode in through the wicket gate past the noticeboard, and began to walk around the churchyard in a frenzy, staring at everything and outraged at everything he stared at.

He drew up short at the foodstuffs, and pointed.

'You can't *do* this!' he said. 'You just can't *do* this. That's my grandfather, that is. What's he doing with all that jam and cake all over him? You'll have to clear him up at once!'

'He won't mind,' Ned explained patiently. 'He won't even know. He's dead.'

'I know he's dead,' said Officer Morton with as much patience as he could muster. 'That's why he's buried here. He's buried here to Rest In Peace, that's what he's buried here for. Not to be bargained over and shopped off by the likes of you.'

Things were going from bad to worse. Ione thought fast.

This had been a very important two weeks for her, in more ways than she had at first realized. She had put a great deal of effort into this sale, and it was the first big thing that she had ever really done.

She wasn't going to give up now. She couldn't. Everything would turn into a waste if she didn't save it. All her work and carrying would go straight down the drain. The other, darker Ned might lose his bullock; but she would lose something too: a gift quite as important and valuable to her as the bullock would be to him. She would lose all the confidence that had been quietly, steadily, secretly growing inside her – confidence that she, Ione Muffet, was capable of real achievements too: that there was always, from now on, going to be more to living for her than just sitting around letting life slide past her.

She could see she had serious thinking to do – about eavesdropping, which was a part of what had got her started on all this, and about lying, which could carry her through even now. Ione promised herself that she *would* think about those things just as soon as she had the time. But right now she was going to take responsibility for rescuing her plans. If trouble followed, then let it. It was worth it to her. And she would try her hardest never to get in this sort of mess again.

Stepping forward, she turned up her clear, innocent face to Officer Morton.

'It's perfectly all right,' she told him calmly. 'There's no problem. We can hold the sale in the graveyard. We have special permission from the Bishop.'

Ned's mouth dropped open.

Caroline said, 'Ooooh,' softly, under her breath.

Officer Morton looked down at Ione, astonished and partly disbelieving.

'You can phone him if you like,' Ione continued coolly. 'To check.'

'Phone the Bishop?'

Officer Morton was appalled by the sheer cheek of the suggestion.

'Certainly,' said Ned, catching on fast. 'I'll get him for you.'

In a flash, he had whipped out his phone and punched in a number.

Ione stood watching. It was her idea, but she was very glad indeed that Ned had taken over.

When the ringing at the other end of the line was broken off by the lifting of the receiver, Ned spoke at once.

'Sorry to disturb you, Your Worship,' he said, 'but we have a bit of a problem here.'

'Is that you, Ned?' said Professor Muffet at the other end. He wished he hadn't answered the phone. He was busy slotting a new cassette into his tape recorder. It had already become jammed twice, and he was getting irritable. He was in no mood for one of Ned's jokes.

'Yes, Your Worship,' said Ned. 'Yes, it is. And we have a problem. Officer Morton would like to be assured that Ione Muffet, a young lady of this parish, does, indeed, have Your Worship's most gracious permission to hold her Grand Bring and Buy Sale in St Edmund's churchyard. On the graves,' he added as an afterthought, in case there should be any confusion. 'Shall I put Officer Morton on the line, Your Worship?'

'No,' said Professor Muffet, fast.

'Here he is, then,' said Ned sweetly, and he handed the phone to Officer Morton, who wiped his palms on the seat of his trousers before taking it gingerly. He held it a safe and respectful distance away from his ear. He could hear strange noises issuing from the other end of the line. These cheap phones do get terrible connections, he thought to himself.

In his study, Professor Muffet was having a wordless, furious tantrum. The things he *gets* me into, he said to himself, wild with anger, sweeping a pile of papers onto the floor. The *trouble* he can be, he added, stamping viciously on the rug. I shall *never* forgive him, he promised himself, tugging frenetically at his thinning hair. I'll *kill* him, he finished up, clenching his fists.

'Your Worship...?' began Officer Morton tentatively.

Professor Muffet consoled himself with the thought that it was a very worthy cause. He calmed himself down at once, just enough to cope.

'Ah, Officer Morton,' Professor Muffet boomed in his most bishoply tones, down the phone. 'So good of you to ring. Most responsible of you to think of checking. I'm extremely pleased with you.'

Officer Morton stood a little straighter, and began to feel better.

'Everything is perfectly in order,' Professor Muffet went on. 'Everyone may carry on. The whole enterprise will bring great credit on the parish of St Edmund's. And it will be appreciated in Higher Quarters, you may be sure of that.' His voice trailed to a halt. Since he had no very clear idea of what was going on down there in the church grounds, he didn't want to get in too deep, in case he set a foot wrong.

Officer Morton remained silent at his end of the phone.

Oh, well, thought Professor Muffet, in for a penny, in for a pound.

'There may even be a photograph,' he ended up blandly. 'I hope to see you in it. You are a credit to the Force.'

Officer Morton swallowed. His heart was very full.

'Thank you, Your Worship,' he said, and gave the phone back to Ned respectfully.

In his study, Professor Muffet cradled the receiver with a bang and went back to his tantrum. But it was no longer a wordless one, and Mandy, overcome with surprise, crept out of the French windows and off into the shrubbery, out of the way.

'That's that, then,' said Ned Hump. 'Back to work, men. It's almost time for the hordes to arrive.'

So Caroline, Ned and Ione quickly went back to work, and Officer Morton slipped back home to polish his shoes and his buttons.

There hadn't been a really *nice* photo of him since the funeral of the Queen Mother, he recalled.

Chapter 22

The Bring and Buy sale was a huge success. Everybody said so. There had never been one to match it in the whole of the village's history. It went on for hours and hours and hours.

Almost everything was sold. What could not be sold was given away. 'It's an ecologically sound principle, recycling is,' said Ned, as he handed Ermyntrude Naseby a broken-off spoon and a pot of ancient jam that nobody had fancied. The jam bore a faint greenish tinge. 'If that doesn't kill you off, you old bat,' he said to her pleasantly, 'then you're immortal.'

'I'll be around to see you hanged, Ned Hump,' she snapped back promptly, and staggered off home, laden with a complete set of new fire irons. 'If I don't do you in myself with these first.'

Mrs Tallentire arrived dead on two-thirty, and

went straight to the books, stacked neatly upon the Hobsons. She rooted through each pile briskly, pulling out one book after another and handing them disdainfully to Ned, who stood attentively behind the grave.

Ned put the books neatly in a cardboard box for her to carry. He thought it was nice of her to have come, after all, and he wanted to be friendly.

'There are thirty-one,' he said, when at last she had checked through every single book pile. 'But because you're taking a whole boxful, I'm going to give you a ten per cent discount.'

'I'm not paying you a single penny,' she informed him. 'However worthy the cause. These books are all lost, mislaid or stolen school books. Every single one of them bears the county stamp.' She narrowed her grey eyes at him suspiciously. 'And I would give a lot to know where they came from.'

'You needn't look at me,' said Ned. '*I* never took them. I never even went to your primary school. I wish I had. But I was educated at home by an extraordinarily beautiful and gifted governess, the natural daughter of an earl. She had golden tresses that fell over my work books in long, soft ringlets, brushing my cheek, and eyes as blue as heaven.' His face took on an expression of rapt remembrance. 'But on my twelfth birthday, she ravished me in the greenhouse and then cut her throat before my very eyes with a pair of gardening shears. So my parents put me in Rutherstrop Technical College.'

Mrs Tallentire shook with irritation.

'You're a *disgrace*,' she whispered at him fiercely. 'An absolute *disgrace*.'

'Can I carry those to the gate for you?' asked Ned pleasantly. 'Whoops, sorry – pardon. *May* I?'

A shiver of scarcely controllable fury passed through Mrs Tallentire's body, and several moments passed before she could collect herself sufficiently to turn on her heel and walk away.

The Waleys came, Ione was pleased and relieved to see. They bought the dog-kennel. Mr Waley proudly tipped it up so his grandson could peep inside.

'There you are, Geoffrey,' he said happily. 'As soon as you've finished teething, we'll get your parents to buy you a puppy so you can get worms instead.'

Ione giggled, and he turned to look at her. 'I've had your poster up,' he told her. 'And everyone remarked on how special it was. Buried the hatchet nicely, didn't we?'

'You'll need another, then,' said Caroline, passing him one around Captain Flook's pillar. 'It's going cheap, because the handle's split.'

'No, thank you,' said Mrs Waley. 'You'd better save it to defend yourself against the vicar when he gets home from his conference and sees all this mess.'

Ione looked around. There was, indeed, a huge amount of mess. There was a huge amount of money, and a huge amount of mess.

'Lovely,' she said to herself, and sighed happily. 'Lovely.'

The graveyard was covered with price tags. They lay over everything, like confetti. A few tattered and soiled napkins still hung from the yew trees, and the ground was spattered with popped red and yellow and blue and green balloon skins.

'How *noisy* it was,' she breathed, thrilled.

It had, indeed, been noisy. One explosion had followed another, like gunfire. The mothers had remonstrated loudly. The children had howled bitterly.

'Just like the Queen Mother's funeral!' Officer

Morton had said to everyone, resplendent in his brushed uniform, gleaming buttons and shiny shoes. He had bought a lovely old doll's house with roses around the door and a peaked red roof for his four-year-old granddaughter's birthday, and Nurse Khan had taken his photo with the camera she had just bought from a grave by the far wall. It was one of those excellent old ones with the adjustable settings, and he could hardly wait to see the prints.

In a lull at the book grave towards the end of the afternoon, Ned wandered over to his vegetable garden.

'Look,' he called to everyone proudly. 'That rain has done it the world of good. The ground's gone all soggy. I think my turnips may shoot up, if it's not too late.'

'Turnips stay down,' said Ione. She was sure someone had told him that before. But he wasn't listening. He had shot off to buy one of the last garden rakes at a knock-down price.

Towards the very end, Professor Muffet had appeared. Mandy picked a way for him, delicately, through the rising debris. With the help of the solicitor's husband, Professor Muffet bought a bottle of Worcestershire sauce off Officer

Morton's grandfather, an oven glove off Martha Cuddlethwaite, and a bright blue ball for Mandy from the war memorial. Then he settled down against a headstone to wait for the sale to finish.

Ione sat in the grass, counting the money. Caroline and Ned leaned back together against the trunk of a cypress and watched the let-go balloons career around the sky in the freshening breeze, like faraway coloured dandelion fluff.

'How wonderful it all was,' said Caroline happily. 'It's going to take us *hours* to clean it all up.'

Ned gave Caroline a hard squeeze. There was dirt all over her hands, stickers all over her hair, and the heavy bruise from yesterday on her cheek. Her nails were all broken, from knotting the balloons. She looked positively scruffy again.

'Oh, well,' she whispered to him, seeing his look, and he kissed her.

Two small children rooted through the undergrowth, looking for lost coins. Their mothers, tired, laden but contented, called to them from the gate. It had been a grand Bring and Buy sale. The best ever.

Ione counted out the piles of money one last time, and tipped them, one by one, into the red cash box.

'It's an absolutely *huge* amount,' she said to them all triumphantly. 'Enough for a *herd* of bullocks, not just one.'

Caroline did the arithmetic. 'Four and three quarter bullocks,' she announced. 'Almost exactly.'

'Only a bit short of *five*, then,' said Ione. She looked around at them all hopefully.

A silence fell.

Everyone stared at Professor Muffet, as if by sheer chance. Even Mandy grew uncomfortable, and shuffled around on her haunches against the headstone.

'Don't,' said Professor Muffet, pushing her down flat. 'Have some sense of where you are.'

Nobody else spoke, and after a few moments, Ned began to whistle softly.

'Are you all looking at me?' Professor Muffet demanded hotly at last. 'Why are you all looking at me? You *are* all looking at me, aren't you? I'm being *looked* at.'

'If the cap fits, wear it,' said Caroline.

'What do you want?' Ione's father insisted. 'What are you waiting for?'

'We're waiting for you to do the decent thing,' said Ned.

'What's that?'

'To cough up.'

'*What?* Pay the *difference?* All by *myself?* Why *should* I?'

'Don't be cheap, please,' said Ned.

They all fell, once again, into another, equally uncomfortable silence.

After a while, Professor Muffet asked:

'Why does it have to be exactly enough for one last whole bullock? Why can't Ione send in what she's got? They can buy the first four, and have some cash left over to buy them some food.'

'Or pretty bells to go around their necks,' said Caroline sarcastically.

Professor Muffet shifted uneasily against the cool stone.

'Maybe they could get a baby one with the left-over pounds,' he suggested.

'Or a deformed one,' said Ned. 'I bet a three-legged bullock can be had for peanuts.'

'Don't be silly,' said Ione. 'It would never stay up.'

Ned stared at her. But since she was staring back at him, equally forcefully, he changed his mind and carried on staring at Professor Muffet instead.

'We're still waiting,' he said sternly.

Professor Muffet thought. Then he went all cunning.

'Couldn't we split it between us?' he wheedled. 'Each of us put in a share. That wouldn't be too much of a blow.'

'Look,' said Ned patiently. 'Try thinking of it this way. If you cough up the missing loot, that means the last bullock is more yours than anyone else's. So you can choose which bit you want. Have the head. The head's the best bit. That's the bit that counts.'

'Not with bullocks,' said Ione.

'It's brawn they want bullocks for, not brains,' agreed Caroline.

Ned waved at them to keep quiet.

'If you have the head,' he said to Professor Muffet, who was still patting nervously at the pocket in which he kept his cheque-book, 'then you can choose its name. See?'

'You could give it *your* name,' said Ione.

'Bullock Muffet,' Ned said in a rich and resonant voice. 'Bullock Muffet. Now that's a fine name for an animal.'

'It is, isn't it?' said Professor Muffet, pleased all at once with the idea. 'It does sound grand, doesn't it?'

'It certainly does,' Ned said firmly. 'And that settles it, then. You can pay by cash or cheque, as you prefer.'

Professor Muffet reached resignedly for his cheque-book, and handed it to Ione, who borrowed a pen from Caroline and wrote in everything before passing it back to her father for him to sign.

Professor Muffet signed with slightly more of a flourish than usual. He was very taken indeed with the idea of a bullock, a huge lumbering tough bullock, rambling around some hot plain on the other side of the world, bearing his name.

He ripped out the cheque, and held it out to them. Ned took it, and handed it, with a low bow, to Ione.

'There you are, Ione,' he said. 'Congratulations. You did it.'

Ione smiled up at him. He had been such a great help. She turned to smile at Caroline. Towards the end she'd been invaluable, too. Then she slipped her hand into her father's, and together they set off down the gravel path towards the church gate.

Every now and again, on the short walk back home, Professor Muffet squeezed his daughter's hand proudly. From time to time he muttered, 'Bullock Muffet,' to himself softly, under his breath.

Ione walked home by his side in a daze of pride and delight, carrying the cash box. The other, darker Ned would not have long to wait now. The rains would fall where he lived, too, in the end, and his land would be tilled and planted. Later, his family would stuff themselves stupid with the long-hoped-for grain.

Ione had plenty of things she should think about. And she would, but not now – not today.

She looked up and around her happily. All along the way, caught and tangled in the horse chestnut trees her mother had planted, the gorgeous fat helium balloons from her Bring and Buy sale strained in the wind to escape and sail gloriously up into the sky.

ABOUT THE AUTHOR

Anne Fine was born in Leicester. She went to Wallisdean County Primary School in Fareham, Hampshire, and then to Northampton High School for Girls. She read Politics and History at the University of Warwick and then worked as an information officer for Oxfam before teaching (very briefly!) in a Scottish prison. She started her first book during a blizzard that stopped her getting to Edinburgh City Library and has been writing ever since.

Anne Fine is now a hugely popular and celebrated author. Among the many awards she has won are the Carnegie Medal (twice), the Whitbread Children's Novel Award (twice), the Guardian Children's Literature Award and a Smarties Prize. She has twice been voted Children's Writer of the Year at the British Book Awards and was the Children's Laureate for 2001-2003.

She has written over forty books for young people, including *Goggle-Eyes*, *Four Babies*, *Bill's New Frock*, *The Tulip Touch* and *Madame Doubtfire*. She has also written a number of titles for adult readers, and has edited three poetry collections.

Anne Fine lives in County Durham and has two daughters and a large hairy dog called Harvey.

www.annefine.co.uk

aNNe FiNe

The Book of the Banshee

It's war...

Will has two sisters.
Muffy – a little angel who loves bedtime stories.
And Estelle.
A screaming, screeching banshee whose moods
explode through the household.
Mum and Dad have surrendered.
And Will feels as if he's living on the front line...

A hilarious tale from multi-award-winning author
Anne Fine.

'Anne Fine has a subversively wicked gift for
exploring family tensions' INDEPENDENT

0 552 55303 4

www.**kids**at**randomhouse**.co.uk

ANNE FINE

The Granny Project

Blackmail – or negotiation?

Mum and Dad reckon things would be better if
Granny were in a Home.
The kids all want her to stay.
Ivan's Granny Project should make his parents
think again.
But there's more than one way of doing a project –
and blackmail can work two ways...

A savagely funny tale from multi-award-winning
author Anne Fine.

Shortlisted for the Guardian Children's Fiction
Award.

'Clever, funny and thoughtful' TLS

'Both audacious and heart-warming' NEW STATESMAN

0 552 55438 3

www.kidsatrandomhouse.co.uk